MW01488192

DOUBLE AGENT

Chris Panos

PublishAmerica

Baltimore

First printing

ISBN: 1-59129-469-X
PUBLISHED BY PUBLISHAMERICA BOOK
PUBLISHERS
www.publishamerica.com
Baltimore

Printed in the United States of America

Dedication

To my beloved wife, Earnestine, who has stood by me faithfully. "Who can find a virtuous woman? her price is far above rubies. The heart of her husband doth safely trust in her.... She will always do him good...." Proverbs 31: 10-12.

To John H. Osteen—my Pastor, Friend, Brother, who stuck with me through thick and thin for nearly forty years.... There is a friend who sticketh closer than a brother....When I was low once John reached out his hand and helped me up... John H. Osteen was a great man of compassion....

CONTENTS

Foreword

by Pat Boone

Double Agent a true-life account of a man, Chris Panos, yet it reads like fiction. It is another "best-seller" in the making. You will not be able to put Double Agent down. It is a story of a man who risked his life behind the Iron and Bamboo Curtains. Chris Panos is a Spy for God.

Double Agent is a sequel to *God's Spy,* a best-seller. This book will help the reader to step forward into new heights. *Double Agent* has a unique style written for the cross-over market. It will thrill you as you read the exciting escapes. Why live a boring life when you can live a supernatural life? It will reveal KGB up-to-date duplicity and their secret technology used against the West.

Introduction

by Chris Panos II

Being an Agent of the Most High God. It has been a great privilege to be called by God. His life has been a miracle. He wouldn't have wanted it any other way. This is the book you have been waiting for. It is going to change your life.

Double Agent is fiction; names, places, and geography have been changed to protect the innocent. The events in this book are based on actual accounts that reflect the reality of a God that intervenes in lives. Chris can attest to it. He has moved in and through his life.

I know you will enjoy this book.

Who is Chris Panos?

by Earnestine Panos

A newborn babe was birthed. He was to be named Petro, after his grandfather, a Greek Orthodox priest. He was born dead, with mucous in his lungs. However, God intervened and spoke to his mother, Catherine, in a vision: "Don't name him Petro but Christos, after Christ."

Then the physician, Dr. Cook, reached down, took the dead baby in his hands, put a hose in the baby's mouth, and drew the mucous from its lungs. He turned the baby on its side and gave it spank on the rear and life was infused into little Christos. He was alive! Chris went through the process of growing up into a young man and later married me, the one whom he says is the love of his life. In his early years, he didn't just think about God, he knew God—he had seen Him in a park when he was 9 years old. At that time, he served as an altar boy in the church. He was touched by God, maybe saved as a child, but he had no teaching of the Gospel to grow in the Lord.

Later, Chris was facing death because of an automobile crash in Houston, Texas. The ambulance had rushed him to Bellaire Hospital but he was lifeless, not expected to live. However, the Lord Jesus Christ appeared to him and laid His hand on Chris. The Lord said, "Chris Panos, I have called you to preach my Gospel into all the World."

Chris Panos came out of that hospital a changed man. He joined the Church and began to read the Bible at 3:00 A.M. every day before going to work. He was a homebuilder at that time. He loved the Word and would spend hours studying it. Soon after, Chris felt God calling him into the ministry. He left his business to follow Jesus with such a love for the Word of God.

In the early 60's, he began to hear that it was impossible to reach the Iron and Bamboo Curtain countries. They were being denied the Word of God. Chris started to pray: "God send me." He asked the Lord to send him where no one wanted to go. God did. Thus, Chris traveled many times behind the Iron and Bamboo Curtain countries. His cargo was the Word of God—Bibles. He experienced many supernatural feats of God. God has blinded customs guards as Chris smuggled Bibles through airports.

Chris was a pioneer in the 10/40 window with the motto: "There are no closed doors to the Gospel." He was going to the 10/40 countries when it was not popular. He was one of the men who paved the way—a pace setter, carving a new road way into nations that were closed to the Gospel.

In India, the first to hold a crusade in Varanasi on the river Ganges, Philip Abraham wrote that many Christian have been killed. Phillip said, "If you come to Varanasi, you must come prepared to die." The power of the devil was broken and on last day Sunday, 100,000 in one service were embracing Jesus Christ as their savior. The vice chairman of the medical school wanted Chris to teach the students how to have faith to heal the sick.

Chris Panos was instrumental in starting the Charismatic movement in Mangalore (200,000 people in one service were crying "We want Jesus"). Archbishop Arokisaswamy of the Roman Catholic Church thanked Chris Panos for coming to India and said: "Everyone could sense that you are fully committed to Christ, and like the Apostle Paul, you were eager to preach Christ and Him crucified. I am extremely happy about the miracle life crusade you conducted here in Bangalore. You made it plain from the beginning that the Holy Spirit alone does these miracles."

As Chris's wife for 48 years, I have stood in the background and viewed many amazing things. Now I am convinced that Chris has been planting seeds and others have been reaping. I know all this because God is not unjust to forget his servant's works and "your labor of love which you have made known in His Name, for you have ministered to the saints and still do minister" (Hebrews 6:10).

We appreciate all your prayers and love gifts that made it possible to reach the lost in many nations all over the world. For more information about Chris Panos' books, tapes, and CD's, go to www.chrispanos.com or write P.O. Box 3333, Houston, TX. 77253-3333.

Chapter 1

Double Agent

It was May 1991. My wife, Earnestine, and I were aboard a Boeing 747. I was on a flight back to Moscow. I could hear the roar of the jet engines. Thoughts reminded me of the many fantastic experiences like blinding the customs agent's eyes and walking unscathed through customs repeatedly. Thoughts were racing through my mind of what would take form for me when I arrived in Moscow.

The weathermen were forecasting a storm of all storms to hit the Soviet Nation by late that evening. No matter how many flights we arranged into Russia, it was always questionable—storms, getting caught at customs, or a host of other fears that we found lurking around every corner. Still, it was exciting times.

I laughed to myself. Here I sat, just one tiny little preacher from Houston, Texas, an avowed Bible smuggler at that, and now receiving an express invitation from Boris Yeltsin, one top leader of the Soviet Union. Quite an accomplishment, even if God was making my introductions.

"So what's on the agenda, Chris?" asked Earnestine, uneasy over something.

We were flying high above the clouds at 33,000 feet. I turned and peered out the window at what could have been the snow fields of Antarctic wilderness. The serenity quieted the soul. It was like you were a little closer to God. "He sent word that he's very excited about meeting with us." I turned to meet her gaze. "He will be picking us up at the airport. After that, we'll meet with the publishing company." I shrugged and tried to smile. "You know the rest. It was another busy week of smiles and tug-of-war interrogation."

Knowing the situation, and who 'he' was, she didn't buy the smile, and few things caught her unprepared lately. It was the same man who had contacted us offering his help. She looked over with that familiar but apprehensive expression. She said, "How are you feeling about 'him'?"

"My hunch is the same."

"Which is?"

"I'm unsure where Menshikov's allegiance lies."

How does a defector from the Baptist Church in Moscow know so much about my life? I call him a defector. I have no proof, but my hunch is the same. My coal black eyes tensed. I knew her reason for asking.

"Well, we're here to meet the publishers and sell the book." She tried to smile. "However, I know you have good reason for concern," she added.

"Yes." Why are they interested in the book now? A book that could easily incriminate many faithful Christians who incidentally have lived through the printing of it in other languages?

"Look at what a tool it could become if they can buy it over the counter. You must take great precautions to protect the names of the participants."

Her words were attempts to relieve me. I nodded an affirmation and rested my head back against the seat. It was never easy doing business with The KGB. Especially when you did not know who they were, or which disguise they were hiding behind that particular day. Menshikov, or any good spy in his secret life, was hidden from the public. He knew too much about me, and I had no idea what he looked like. I had only talked with him on a static-ridden phone.

Two flight attendants busied themselves toward the middle of the plane. An older gentleman was making a royal nuisance out of himself. He was asking for cold coffee and salty peanuts in a very annoying way.

Obviously he had not traveled too often. I laughed at his surprised look when the flight attendant dumped three ice cubes into his drink and marched off down the aisle.

I meditated over Earnestine's question. How did I feel about Menshikov? More important, how and why had he gotten himself involved? For me to get a nod from a Russian publisher at all, at this time, was not a mere chance. It was Divine Providence to get the invitation from Yuri. It put me in contact with the right people at the publishing company. This was an opportune time. I felt like having a special party.

The flight went as planned. Earnestine read her book; I studied people. The closer we got to Russian soil, the more the plane rocked and reeled. I looked around at my fellow passengers. The majority looked uneasy. An older woman sitting a seat away was airsick. I knew sickness came about because of the storm. Or was it a work of the devil adding to my surroundings? Suddenly a voice came on the intercom requesting we fasten our seatbelts. Like an early peek at daybreak, I suddenly saw the lights of Moscow on the horizon.

"Are you ready for this?" asked Earnestine as she organized her belongings in preparation to land.

"Ah, my child. Where is your faith?"

The landing was perfect, but the moment our feet touched ground, it was frozen ice, and a gust of arctic air blasted. It took our very breath away. Hearty groans washed over the crowd as they ran for cover. We wanted warmth and security behind closed doors. I must say that in the winter in Russia, staying warm is hard. You wake up cold. You go to bed cold. The time between is spent slapping your hands together. Inside the confines of the terminal, we headed toward the baggage area. Dark penetrating eyes watched from a distance.

"You're uptight about something," said Earnestine as we walked past two uniformed guards.

"I've been doing my homework on Menshikov. I was trying to understand why his grandfather, an intricate part of the Russian Army, had a grandson who joined the Russian Baptist Church."

Earnestine didn't have an answer. Neither did I. She excused herself and headed for the powder room. I dug in my pocket for the baggage stubs.

"Mr. Panos?" came a colorful voice from behind me.

"Yes?" I wheeled around to see who had spoken. Some nicely-dressed good person stood quietly examining me more than passively.

"You must be Chris?"

My first consideration, even though he had used my first name, was that this man might have been more at home at a swank New York party scene. He could be running a casino for the Mafia in Las Vegas. Earnestine approached just as they formally introduced him. The smile was friendly, but reserved.

"My name is Yuri Menshikov. I assume you are the man I have been waiting here for?"

"Why might you assume that?"

"They told me to look for a short man with a big smile. They also said he would be in the company of his dear wife." He looked over at Earnestine. "I think that fits your description." He smiled skeptically.

The man was impeccably dressed. Every hair was in place. In a country where money was scarce and usually only provided by government employment, he seemed richly dressed and groomed. I stepped back to evaluate the man dispensing his words with such gusto, and trying to impress me with his command of the English language.

His smile suddenly looked genuine, a part of his facade I found out later, but for the moment I was grateful. "Please excuse the lateness. The traffic's terrible," he said as he motioned us toward the large corridor.

My cautious resignation went by unnoticed. Several pairs of eyes watched from a distance. A well-dressed man in civilian clothes lurked around the far side of the corridor. He walked like a man with counterfeit motives. You could hear the roaring lions in the background and I felt like I could give him a slip in the zoo because there were so many people there.

Then I got the idea to start following Menshikov. After years of smuggling Bibles and playing the hide-n-seek with the KGB, I was seldom at a total loss for words, but I couldn't shake the feeling of distrust for the well-dressed gentlemen.

"I understand that you tried, in the past, to get your book published?" he said, jumping into the middle of my thoughts.

"The book has been published in many other languages—just not in Russia, for obvious reasons."

His brow lifted. "And what do you speculate now?"

"Possibly—if the timing is right." I was not ready to commit myself. Only God knew the answer. He shifted his attaché case from one hand to the other and motioned for us to take a sharp turn to the right.

"About your book," he said again, as he nodded to several people who knew him. "I am quite honored to be meeting you. I have read your book."

"The book has garnered a great measure of success, but let me set you straight on one thing. It's God's book, not mine."

I looked at the man with the barren expression. Who was he, and why was he here? "My prayer, Mr. Menshikov, is that it will come to fruition in your country at this time..."

"Which is why I agreed to set up a meeting with Conicom Publishing Co., the largest publishing company in Russia, but it was only after I read the book."

It's an excellent book. He said, "Did you get the meeting set up?"

"It's set."

I waited further for explanation. None came. I had been a businessman much too long not to acknowledge my gut feelings. "Well, no matter how much ground work is laid, a deal is never a deal till it's signed and sealed and the paperwork's complete," I said, pausing, offering him a chance to rebut.

"Final negotiations can make or break any deal."

Chapter 2

Rich Russian Oyster

Menshikov reminded me of some rich Russian oyster, all tucked away nicely in his shell. While our teeth chattered and bit at each other, he was perfectly at home in this arctic Siberia. I had seen cold before, but this was the worst storm on record.

"Mrs. Panos, has the weather snatched your breath away," asked Menshikov, "or are you having second thoughts about this meeting about to take place?" Menshikov pointed us three rows over to his black sedan.

Earnestine hurried on, offering no response, which was very unlike her. As we approached the vehicle, he unlocked the door and stood waiting her answer.

"Well, it's certainly a long way from smuggling Bibles in," she said with candor as she climbed in.

His smile was forced. He said, "This is a great privilege for you. Conicom is one of Russia's oldest publishing companies, and are you excited?"

Suddenly I broke out with laughter. "Yes, I am."

Once we were all safely tucked inside the vehicle, I caught her reflection in the rear view mirror. "I think grave caution might be the right response," I chimed in, giving her a chance of a reprieve. Earnestine had suspicion that we were being set up. "Please understand our hesitation on this," I added. "Even the action heroes of the book are unsure about it being published here in their homeland."

Menshikov started the car with a roar.

"Don't take me wrong," I said. "We are elated about the possibility of this deal, but we have valid reservations, too. How will it affect my ministry? And will it slam the doors shut? The pendulum is swinging in Russia, but many people, including me, remember the days when Bible smugglers were killed or imprisoned for much less."

The parking lot was suddenly full and running over. Menshikov had to push to get a jump ahead of the crowd. "Why did you agree to take it upon yourself to set up this meeting?"

Menshikov stopped the vehicle to allow three elderly gentlemen the opportunity to run across in front of us.

"I made the offer, Mr. Panos, because Conicom happens to be one of Russia's largest publishing companies. I have had dealings... No, let me rephrase that. Since the church has had dealings with them." He raised a hand in explanation. "I know the owners personally."

"Thanks are in order, Menshikov, either to you or to whoever might be responsible." I looked over at him, knowing that I was indeed grateful. This was a gift from God. "Whatever might happen from here, Mr. Panos, I believe congratulations are in order because I have further good news." Menshikov's eyes danced with a secret he had not openly shared with us yet.

"Just being here to negotiate this book is the most exciting news I could possibly ask for," I said with a smile. My mind stretched back over the many years of ministry in the Soviet Block Nations. I recalled how hard I had worked on smuggling Bibles. In my heart I knew the book would come to seed—if it was in God's timing.

"Along with the contract for your book, they've expressed a committed desire for you to appear on Russian radio and TV as well."

"You aren't serious?" I declared in disbelief. We stopped for a traffic jam that was now edging forward a couple of feet at a time. Off to one side I saw a small, nondescript man straining to peer into our vehicle. The flash would have gone by unnoticed except for the bald head. I remembered my friend's remark.

"If that were to happen, Mr. Menshikov, I'd call it a miracle."

"I would not know about that," he said gruffly.

The very thought enthralled me. What an opportunity. The chance to speak to thousands of lost souls who had never before heard the Gospel, and in a way never before permitted in Russia! I looked over at Earnestine, who was wearing a great big smile.

An hour later we walked into our hotel room at the Russian house, an old hotel in the center of Moscow. Earnestine's smile was gone. She was in a world of her own, checking things out, examining things. I made a couple of phone calls. When I hung up, she was still inspecting the room as if she was looking for something.

"Is something wrong?" I asked.

"I'm a little jumpy." She looked around the room.

Usually when Earnestine spoke like this it was in direct relation to a gut feeling she was feeling. Over the years we had learned to pray more when we felt threatened.

"Are you having second thoughts?" I asked.

"Oh, don't mind me, Chris. This is a picnic compared to Bangalore or Shanghai." Her laugh released the tension in the air. A few minutes later she had her wardrobe hung up. I had the scanner attached to the telephone. I could never understand how a place could be so quickly bugged. I called and reserved the room from the airport.

That evening, in advance of the meeting with Conicom, I was going over some paperwork. At first the noise was faint, then I distinctly heard the door knob being turned. I stood up, expecting someone to burst through the door screaming or flashing a pistol to haul us off. When nothing happened, I opened the door. Whoever had been outside my door had fled; the hallway was empty, but in the haste they had dropped something. I leaned over and picked up an ink pen. It was nice one with a red and gold top, easily distinguishable from an ordinary variety. I tucked it away inside my briefcase.

The following day we were up and ready to go early. Menshikov again volunteered to drive us. I didn't turn him down. The trip to the publishing company was uneventful. I didn't learn anything that I didn't already know. I was hoping that Menshikov would prep me on what to say. He didn't.

I pulled up the chair to sit across the table from the men with Conicom. I began negotiating the contract. It seemed that Menshikov was about to say something. After the introduction, he smiled, stood up, and left the room.

Alex Vatuin, the older gentlemen, looked up from his paperwork offering small talk, and again asked my reasons for being here. I wasn't sure he believed my motive.

"We've been exploring the possibility of having a radio and television program such as yours. After careful consideration, we've decided to negotiate an offer with you."

Stunned, and barely able to speak, I stammered, "You're proposing that I have a slot on your station?"

"That, Mr. Panos, is what we are proposing."

Menshikov had broken the news earlier, but I doubted it would actually take form. The two gentlemen weren't waiting for my answer, instead they continued with their paperwork as if this kind of thing happened every day.

"I would be extremely honored," I said, when I found my tongue.

"You will need an interpreter," offered the younger gentlemen, Bosch Tolkachev, a bald, short, pudgy man who spoke with a thick Russian accent. He was sitting next to Earnestine. His smile was contagious and looked genuine. "Since we have access to such, we could provide that for you." The office was so gloomy, dark, and oppressive.

"That is, only if you would like for us to do that," said Alex Vatuin, a slender, handsome, blue-eyed devil, peeking over the tops of his reading glasses again. He had very poor eyesight. His lenses were very thick. This was more service than I was used to getting in my deals with the Russians.

"Who is this interpreter?" I asked.

"She's no novice. She's the anchor person for one of our radio/television stations. She is the tough lady. You will be doing business with her."

"Have you used her in the past?" A thought raced through my mind: *I hope she's well-seasoned and familiar with Americans.*

"We call her our Dianne Sawyer look-a-alike."

He didn't address my question. I faltered, wondering if it was proper to broach a particular subject with these men. After I'd had a moment to think about their offers, I decided to pose a question.

"Since you are so well accomplished at putting together deals, perhaps you could get me an audience with Patriarch Alexis?"

Alex looked up with such distaste, his cordialness suddenly disappeared. "Sir. We're a publishing company, not God Himself." He tossed some papers over my way. "Read these carefully."

"Some people are fortunate enough to get an audience with the Patriarch," I said. I wasn't about to let it lay, but I did begin to read over the paperwork.

He looked up, again peering over his glasses. "There's no way you could get in to see the Patriarch on this short notice, even if your name was Jesus." The words were precise, to the point, exactly as intended. "His meetings are reserved for important heads of state, and they have to make appointments well in advance."

"Oh," I said with an embarrassed shrug as I began to read through the documents. I would accept his reproach for now, but I knew in my spirit that if God was in it, the appointment would come about.

I couldn't believe it. Here were the papers, in my hand, signed, sealed. The quotes, "paperwork" done, a few years past. What could I say? The meeting went better than either of us imagined. We signed a contract to have our book printed in Russian, and with it came the radio and television contract. Two miracles at one time!

The meeting was over, and the papers were tucked neatly away in my coat pocket. I stood to my feet. Alex, the older gentleman, smiled as he pushed himself back in his chair and motioned for me to sit back down. With a scratchy tone to his voice, he looked at me as if he had some expressive words.

"Now, Mr. Panos, I have a real question for you." He paused as if mulling over his question. "Some say you are a member of the CIA—you know, a double agent." He examined my first response. His words went over my head.

"Yes, Mr. Panos, now that we are on some more intimate terms. I would like to know if there is any truth to this." He looked rather embarrassed. "Of course, I am only asking because I have grandchildren at home. It would certainly make for a good bedtime story." He laughed.

I returned his enthusiasm with equal zeal, bending forward as if I were going to divulge my innermost secrets. "But of course, Alex," I said laughing. "And it would be a well-kept secret. You would not mention a word to anyone." I stood to my feet. "After all, you are only a publishing company." I smiled richly and thanked them for the courtesy extended, expressing my heartfelt thanks again before I left.

The contract was signed. The action had not been hasty. Actually, looking back, it had been a rational and well-planned procedure, and, I might add, God-directed; but being human with the faltering human spirit, I had a growing list of questions.

Menshikov reminded me of a scorpion, and hardly fit my image of a mentor.

Would the book actually come to print or was it a plot to get it in their hands to use against my ministry? Did Menshikov actually work for the Baptist Church, or for the KGB?

Chapter 3

A Caller After Dark

After signing the contract for the book, *God's Spy*, I asked, "Why me, God?" It wasn't a complaint but more a humbling of my personality. The deal offered by Conicom Publishing Company was generous. We quickly maneuvered through the fundamental paperwork. Looking at it from the proper perspective, it was two miracles rolled into one; I would be the very first minister given this sort of privilege ever in Russia, and I would be one of the first to go on Russian radio and television.

About the interpreter from Conicom? I declined the offer, wanting to give it some thought. I couldn't put my finger on it at the time, but I felt better not offering an immediate reply. A couple days after the signing, Earnestine and I had been praying and thanking God for the miracle. We continued our petitions to Him for our specific prayer needs: an interpreter. A decision had to be made soon.

One evening we were watching the late news on television when we heard the knock at our door. "Who on earth would be at our door this late?" groaned Earnestine as she rose from her chair.

We approached the door cautiously. Earnestine stood directly behind me. An evening caller after dark in Russia is reason enough to strike fear.

"Hello," said the soft-spoken young lady standing half-hidden in the dimly-lit hall. "My name is Irina Yurchenko. I was told you are looking for an interpreter."

Her dark-framed glasses sat perched atop a perfectly-shaped Roman nose. The face looked sincere enough. I felt something was wrong in my spirit. I must have looked surprised. It was 9:30 p.m., much too late for a young lady to be approaching a stranger's door.

"Pardon me," I said rather skeptically. "Could you tell me who sent you here?" Then I began to scan the empty, dingy, dark hall. Looking behind her, I could see no evidence that she had been accompanied by anyone.

"Oh, I'm sorry." Her accent was heavy. "I hope I'm not disturbing you? Conicom gave me your address. They said you were in need of an interpreter."

"Oh," I said, scanning cautiously, looking at Earnestine.

Her drab tan coat looked like something a reporter would wear. She stood about 5'7", hair pulled back in a bun—not necessary disheveled looking, but she looked like she'd spent a harried day chasing leads.

"They said you would like to talk with me." She pulled her gloves off, holding them in her hand. The hands were a working woman's, rough with shortly manicured nails. I stepped past her out into the hallway and looked both ways before I invited her in. She seemed surprised at our ready acceptance to speak with her. Earnestine shot a vigilant glance my direction as she offered her the chair nearest the door.

"Are you the anchorwoman for Echo Radio Station? The slender woman from Conicom they began speaking to me about?" I asked, noticing her eyes sparkled with interest when I mentioned Conicom. "The publishing company informed me that they had contacts with the radio station's head reporter. Is that you?" A thought flashed through my mind. *She had to be older*.

"No, I'm not," she stammered. "She is not available. I'm sorry, but another pressing assignment came in, one that she has been nurturing for some time." She looked over at Earnestine. "She sends her apology." Her words were administered with care. "If I do not meet your expectations, I can be easily replaced."

"Translate a few sentences for me," I said as I pulled a magazine from the table and began to read. She responded quickly, repeating the words after me, using efficiency. I was fluent enough in Russian to acknowledge she was interpreting. She was able to follow along after me. Whoever sent her had sent a professional.

"How much to retain you?" I asked as I seated myself in the straight-back chair near the table directly across from her. I always liked to face a nervous opponent square-off.

She smiled, her first since entering the room. "I understand that you are a minister with the Greek Orthodox Church."

I nodded—a Greek Orthodox, called by God to spread the Good News.

"Well, I could translate for a nominal fee because of your profession. At times I do accept a lesser fee. I understand people like you are not wealthy."

"What is your nationality? I'm having a difficult time detecting it."

"I'm Armenian." She pulled her coat down over her shoulders.

"Forgive our manners. May we take your coat?"

"No, thank you." She was not interested in giving up her coat, but in one quick movement she opened her pocketbook and retrieved a strange-looking pen, a black one with a red top. It cleared up an immediate question, but opened up several others. I eased back in my chair, evaluating the situation. Since the publishing company was trying so hard to place their spy, I decided to play along. She quoted a fair price. I didn't haggle. After a few minutes of listening to me explain what the meeting would entail, she said she understood.

"Shall I meet you at the radio station?" she asked as she stood up.

"Yes. I've been asked to be available before 7:00 a.m." I ushered her to the door where we said a delicious goodbye.

The moment the door closed behind her, I turned to Earnestine. We knew the meeting was not by chance.

Chapter 4

I Have Roots in Your Country

The following day Irina Yurchenko appeared at the radio station exactly three minutes after Earnestine and I had arrived. We smiled to offer our thanks. We were immediately swept into the meeting room by the staff. The Russian people have little use for social formality and consider it frivolous and unessential.

"Thank you, Mr. Panos, for agreeing to these meetings," said Sergei, the anchorman for the radio station. He looked into the cameras, searching for the right one in which to speak. "I don't think I have to tell you that this is a new venture for this station." He turned facing the audience and the camera.

"I am extremely honored to have a long-time minister and businessman here from America. Would you please welcome our distinguished guest, Chris Panos, from Houston, Texas."

"Thank you, Sergei," I said prayerfully when he turned the microphone over to me, and I began to speak on Russian national radio and television for the very first time. I was humbled and fearful, being the explorer in this unique expedition. There had never been anyone providing examples before, at least not in this category. If my words hit the right chord, God's name would be exalted to the people of Russia.

"I greet you in the name of Jesus Christ. I count it a great privilege to be on this Echo Station of Moscow."

I began to speak. Irina's Yurchenko's look changed as she translated for me. Sergei showed little recognition for the Armenian interpreter who had been engaged for the presentation. She spoke

29

eloquently and quietly as she translated each word. I continued. She followed quickly along, giving the correct interpretation. Even the verbiage was precise. Her words denoted loyalty to Jesus Christ. I was praying that God would anoint each word that she spoke as she translated the words of peace and deliverance to the Russian people.

The meeting offered the radio audience an in-depth look at me and my ministry. Most of all it offered a first-hand introduction to the man who heals broken hearts: Jesus Christ.

Sergei's interview was informative. He asked all the right questions a professional reporter would have asked, aiming the questions at me, via the expertise of Irina, which she in turn directed toward the Russian audience. I understood most of the interpretation. I recalled President George Bush and Prime Minister Indira Gandhi of India, both friends of mine, said they knew enough different languages to know when they were getting an introduction, being praised, or being fooled. I felt I had that same ability of discernment.

Directing my interests to Sergei, the tall, handsome gentleman with thinning blond hair and a bushy handlebar mustache, giving him a somewhat Victorian appearance, I couldn't help but think he didn't fit the stereo type of a KGB Operative. I wondered, in my heart, if he truly was closely tied to the Communist Party or if he was considering the same as an alternative question for me.

"It's remarkable," I said, leading him forward, "how God has opened doors for me to meet world leaders, kings, and priests. It's one of the most exciting times of my life, being here with you, addressing the Russian people." I appraised the finely-dressed gentleman who sat before me.

"We have heard great things of you, Mr. Panos. Tell us about yourself. The Russian people know very little."

"Mine is a unique story," I said, directing my gaze toward the camera. The studio was compact but well-equipped. In fact, the quarters were cramped. We had to scoot around one another when a point was made, yet the anointing of God was powerful and I said, "My grandmother came from Russia. Did you know that?"

His brows lifted.

"Her name was Elena Korniloff. She was the niece to Alexander II, cousin to Alexander III, and aunt to Nicholas II." If that wasn't enough political clout, I thought to myself, possibly I should have brought an entourage. "My grandfather was a tutor in the Czar's household. He took her away from Russia during the turbulent times. They went to Greece. He wanted to marry her, and he eventually did. So you see, even though I am an American, and I come to you from far across the world, I have roots in your country."

Would this information be accepted by the average Russian, or would they disbelieve what I was saying? How hard is it for a people who are forced to lie for the sake of the government to believe such a story?

"Allow me to offer you my sincere appreciation for this opportunity. I feel very privileged to be in this great nation of Russia. I came to encourage Russia." And I turned, facing the in-house audience and Sergei. "Life has a strange way of changing and rearranging itself. What is absolute today may be changed tomorrow, but God does not change—and I will add that the best is yet to come."

Sergei's eyes acknowledged his acceptance of my well-thought-out statements.

"As a businessman in Houston, Texas, over the years I became a developer, a builder, and I was in real estate. We built developments, houses, and shopping centers. Money was easily attainable for me, and through development deals, I made much money, but my heart was empty."

The words coming out of my mouth struck an empty chord in my heart. "You see, I didn't know where I belonged." I calculated each word. In the flashes of seconds between my words and those of the interpreter, I thought back to those days when my heart had felt so empty. Irina Yurchenko glanced my way, waiting for me to continue.

"I attended the Greek Orthodox Church. My grandfather was a Greek Orthodox priest, but even so, I did not truly understand that Jesus Christ was my Savior."

Irina Yurchenko was young and not easily swayed. As I shared my close call with death and the events that surrounded my coming to the Lord, I felt the coolness in her spirit to the subject. As an intellectual, I could tell she did not believe the words she was translating, but her rendering never faltered.

"God loves all people. That's the key," I said. "The key is Jesus, the good news is the Gospel." I searched my heart for the right words—remembering how I learned about this Savior. "After I accepted the reality of a savior, Jesus Christ, in my heart and not in my head." I used my hands in describing what I was relating, "and believed on him... I was born again... not because I became good, or because I deserved it, but it is because I believed in Jesus, God's only son."

I spoke one-on-one with the audience, as if I had just walked into their living room. My words painted a picture. The Bibles, smuggling them in, and the daring exploits and escapes. Irina appeared preoccupied, looking away at times as if she was detached from the words she was relaying. I couldn't tell if she was being touched by the message at times, or if she was looking at the clock on the wall behind my head. "The Bible said God would come out of the heavens and walk with man—in the cool of the day. There was a great communion between man and God."

With those words came a sweet peace sent to all who heard. I envisioned God, up in His heaven, coming down to walk with man.

"When God created man, there were three things he never intended man to do." The cameramen, stage hands, and Sergei were spellbound, listening very intently to my every word. Irina, translating the words, looked directly into my eyes as she tried to stay ahead of me.

"There were three things God never intended for man to do," I said again as I shifted in my seat. The words were going to be profound. Then the cameramen were quietly poised, waiting for me to go on. God impressed me that very moment that many would hear this day about an almighty God for the very first time in their lives. Some would be inspired to delve deeper, possibly to go far enough to accept a personal invitation to accept him into their hearts. I knew that as a truth, in my spirit, as much as I knew my own name. It was the reason God had preordained that I am in this place, at this moment, to speak the words of life to them.

"Ladies and gentlemen, listen to me," I said. "Number one. God never intended for man to sin. Number two. God never intended for man to be sick. And lastly, God never intended for man to die."

The camera zoomed in to pick up my facial expression. I, of all men, knew how impossible it is for sinful man to somehow know godly principles. We read books on literature, science, history. We easily receive the wisdom they have to offer. But all the books in the world cannot bring real wisdom. That wisdom comes only from God, the creator of our universe, of our galaxy, and all the galaxies in the far reaches of the heavens.

At that moment I could have said anything and it would have been accepted. "I respect all churches and honor them. God has a message. He called me to go and tell the world that He 'IS'. It is so very simple."

As the words became alive, I was moved within my own heart. *God 'IS,'* I thought, *and he talks with me, as he expresses with everyone within my hearing.* He is no repecter of persons. He talks with all humans.

"God loves you," I said as I turned to face the camera. "God loves you," I repeated gently. As I lifted my eyes, I could feel what God was saying to my spirit. I knew from the facial expressions around me. God was dealing with them.

Chapter 5

Patriarch Alexei's

Over the following days, I wrestled with an idea. I said, "Well, God, you've given the signing of the contract for the book and you've miraculously opened doors to Russian radio and television. What could be next?"

I felt, in my spirit, God was pressing me to give the church a percentage of earnings that I gained from the book. The next thing needed was to meet with the Patriarch, the overseer of the Russian Orthodox Churches, to outline the contractual vow.

It's impossible to get an audience with the Patriarch, Paul and the others said. I wondered if they had joined forces with the publishing company. "No one can see the Patriarch without an appointment. It takes weeks in advance, especially if they are involved with other things," said another.

I had no idea what was involved. I didn't involve myself in a mental maneuver. Earnestine and I went back to our room to pray for contacts to get us through to see the Patriarch.

"Lord, help us," I said as we prayed in our hotel room. "Our contacts don't seem to be working. Lord, what we need is a breakthrough."

Suddenly the thought came to me to take my press kit to the travel agent inside the hotel, who happened to speak Greek, and visit with her. It was as if God was saying, "She will work with you."

I did as I was instructed. Earnestine stayed behind to continue to pray. Just as I rounded the corridor into the main foyer, I stepped in behind a little old couple. The lady in charge was too busy with them to take notice of me.

The plaque on her desk displayed the name Margot Kryuchkov, but the nameplate on her front pocket read Margot. On my first evaluation, I found her to be firm-jawed and well-tailored, definitely all business. By American standards, she was not pretty, but there was an attractiveness in the way she carried herself as she moved from one area of the desk to another. I entertained myself by flipping through an old magazine I'd found lying close by.

The little couple doing business with her was refusing to elaborate on an answer when she posed a question at them. They probably worked for the KGB, I thought. Besides these tactical observations, I had no other evidence. Ten minutes later, and a little weary from waiting, I stepped up to the desk.

"Hello," I said with a smile that radiated across my face. "Seems you've had your hands full." My eyes followed the little couple down the hall.

"I'm used to conflicting loyalties," she said with finality, as if dusting her hands of the responsibility.

We made small talk. I felt it was important to build trust, a rare commodity in Russia. I had confidence God could accomplish it. Her dark hair tied back in a bun was accented by the almost ebony-black eyes, striking at first glance, but almost without eyelashes. I handed her one of my business cards, then my press kit that was chock full of pictures of President George Bush, Patriarch Athenagroas, Archbishop President Makarios of Cyprus and others.

"What's this?" she asked with a questioning glance as she tried to read the name.

"I'm down here because God told me to come down and give you this." I handed her my book, *God's Spy*, which she accepted. She was still looking puzzled, but began flipping through its pages. She went back and reread the name on the front.

"Please call the Patriarch's office and ask him for an appointment." I felt limited. How do you convince a possible KGB agent to help further the Gospel? In my experience, most travel agents and airline attendants were KGB officers. The thought came from God, and I began speaking. "I have a message and a gift for him," I explained.

She looked at me with great suspicion. Margot was of the old Communist school, the kind who anticipated every event as an external threat. A few more minutes of small talk, and after a time of agreement with herself, she reluctantly reached over and picked up the phone.

I silently watched as she roared through one contact after another. Within a half an hour she put the phone back down and smiled, the first one I'd seen so far, but I wasn't sure how genuine it was.

"You have an audience with the Patriarch for 7:00 p.m. tomorrow evening." She handed me the piece of paper with the details.

In less than forty minutes she had accomplished something the publishing company said could not be done. "Thank you," I said graciously.

She was hesitant to accept this genuine thank you. It showed in her eyes, the expression reflecting years of distrust. I wondered what I might give her in return for the favor. I wanted to repay her kindness somehow.

There was interest in my problem that was not in line with the party's bureaucracy. Margot was openly examining me as a real person.

"Could you order me a Lincoln Continental limousine?"

Startled, she said hesitantly, "What color?" She was unsure if I was serious or not.

I thought about it a minute. "White," I said, considering my reason. "It seems the fitting color for a man of God. Don't you think?" I was thinking out loud. "You don't go to meet a President, Prime Minister, or a King with patches on your pockets. It's not the time to be humble."

"Protocol I understand, Mr. Panos."

"Actually, I did forget about protocol once," I said, leaning over on her desk, which was just about arm level.

"You owe me no explanation," she said, adapting her personality and conversation to what was expected, still trying not to be too dogmatic. It was easy to see that she had learned to do and say one thing while thinking something else. Obviously she had been used as a tool to further the cause, but I doubted she had any idea of how mechanical she had become within its framework.

"Thank you so much for getting through the red tape. Possibly I will do a favor for you sometime."

She smiled, looking embarrassed, obviously unaware of how to handle a gentle word as she grabbed for the phone that had started to ring. I waved a goodbye. I was exuberant about what had just transpired.

The Russian House, was an old hotel, but beautiful. The lobby was filled with little shops selling little dolls of Gorbachev and Yeltsin. The travel agency was in the lobby. The people were busy as bees swarming in and out of the hotel. I wanted to shout and run up the stairs to tell Earnestine. "You won't believe what just happened... We have an audience with the Patriarch tomorrow evening!" I said as I slammed through the door.

"Oh, Praise the Lord!" she said with a gasp.

"But we still need the interpreter."

"What about Irina Yurchecko, the Armenian interpreter we engaged for the radio and television presentation?"

I paced the length of the room and back in a circle.

"She's worked with you previously. You know it would at least be workable." Earnestine's eyes followed me around the room and I paced the length again. My gut feelings were the same as before.

"I'm not sure. It was very convenient of Conicom to send her over under the pretense that the Diane Sawyer look-alike had other engagements."

"She did a good job for you."

"I can't put my finger on it..."

"It's late, Chris." Earnestine looked at the clock on the long, extended dresser. "I'm not sure you can come up with another interpreter on such short notice, at least one that could cover it and get it all set in time. She even gave you her phone number."

"I know. It adds to my suspicion," I said, thinking on it a few minutes before I relented and called. Irina and I talked briefly, going over the basics. I asked her to meet us at the hotel the following evening. I explained that we would be leaving in a limousine from the Russian House Hotel promptly the following day.

Chapter 6

Irina, Long Silky Legs

The meeting was set. The following evening my now-famous interpreter, Irina Yurchenko, arrived at the hotel. We left for the cathedral. As soon as she appeared I could see a dramatic change.

Irina Yurchenko no longer wore the drab tan trench coat with her frazzled hair all tied up in a bun. Even Earnestine's eyes protruded when the lovely Irina arrived on the scene in a black, sleek dress, cut high enough to show off her long, shapely legs. The hair was freshly shampooed and cascading about her face like tufts of cotton candy. I say this with much prudence. Irina looked ravishing.

She bounded through the door flashing an experienced smile and extending a hearty hello. You would have thought she met the Patriarch every day. The moment her dark eyes caught my attention, I was reminded of the words of warning: "We can arrange for a beautiful young Russian girl to fall in love with one of our visitors." I had been told these words before, but I had shoved the warning aside, more intent on the goal before me. I was in God's perfect will.

We had been waiting only a couple minutes when the big white limousine pulled up outside of the Russian House. I didn't wait for the door to be opened for us. Instead, I stepped forward and opened the door for two ladies. Irina slid into the seat that faced backward. Earnestine and I crawled into the back seat that put us facing to the front, directly across from each other. He closed the doors.

"Irina, so, you have never been into the cathedral before now?" I asked as the driver took off with a jerk.

"I have no reason to go. I am a good Russian," she said with an accomplished smile as her eyes circled the vehicle and came back to rest on mine.

Earnestine was her usual bubbly self. She was very excited about the meeting. I had a feeling I was being set up. The driver said something in Russian. Irina laughed and tossed her head to the side, answering pertly. After a few more invitational questions and rebuttals, she turned around and spoke directly to him in Russian. He returned the favor, words obviously tossed out in jest and meant for her ears only, and they both broke into laughter. I looked out the window enjoying the landscape. Earnestine and I had spent a lot of time in Russian but there was always more to see. I guess my mind drifted to another scene when we were in St. Petersburg, Russia. I was at Isaiah's Cathedral. It was immaculate. Then we journeyed to the River Neva, which brought back memories about the summer palace. Wow, what a man Peter the Great was, who started to build this magnificent city. You could see Peter's dream unfolding as he built the canals that separate the Italian-inspired buildings. The Annunciation Cathedral was built in 1489. Speaking of the cathedrals, the Patriarch's cathedral of Moscow was incredible. The gold dome sparkled in the sunlight. You could visit the Czars within the cathedral and see the inspiring frescoes of the saints and church history painted on the walls. They seemed to come to life and project the compassionate Christ that died on the cross. It was breathtaking. One fresco caught my attention. It was in the Book of Revelation. The fifth seal was opened and painted on the southern wall and on the western wall the Prophet, Elias, fighting the Antichrist, a four-legged animal. Suddenly we hit a bump in the road. It took me away from my thoughts and I heard Irina talking in the limousine.

Irina continued to carry on her conversation with the driver, privately and almost in whispers, for the span of a few miles. They laughed occasionally. I felt fairly confident in my ability to make my wishes known in Russian, but whatever language they were speaking must have been another dialect. I couldn't understand but only some of it.

Upon surrendering to the Lord, I was surprised to find that the commerce of the world was seldom carried out on Godly principles. Far from it. In fact, my first step in religious education was to learn the language of the larger world, so I could incorporate our Lord Jesus' language of metaphors of the simple people into a workable language. I found that his message of love was universal. Irina's message was universal, too, but depicting a different kind of love.

Finally, Irina turned back around to face us. As if on the cue, she threw back her head and laughed, seductively brushing the hair back away from her face in the same move. As if in slow motion she lifted one long, silky leg over the top of the other, indiscreetly trying to gain recognition and composure. It wasn't so much what she did as how she accomplished it.

She reminded me of an athlete. For their own purpose of strength conditioning, they know to increase ability and agility it takes hard work and practice. Irina had practiced her skills. I surveyed the situation, feeling tense.

"What was the limo driver saying to you?" I asked.

She giggled. "Oh, he wants to make a date with me." She laughed again, flashing her most beautiful smile, which looked innocent enough till she coupled it with her body language that portrayed something different. I actually felt embarrassed at her actions. Earnestine was making her own observations and deductions. Irina was an attractive person. She was no comparison to Earnestine. Earnestine had a sparkle of joy in her eyes as we walked into the Patriarch's Cathedral.

I knew without a shadow of doubt, at that very moment, why Irina Yurchenko had been assigned to me. Over the years I had spent a lot of time away from Earnestine out doing God's work. There were times when I was forced to pray for Godly wisdom and spiritual guidance, and he had always been there to guide me through, but never had I been openly enticed in front of my wife. The devil must have been getting anxious to catch me in a fault.

Earnestine looked in my direction, offering consolations. I understood at that moment what some of the more outspoken critics meant when they said, "In the utter confusion of the modern world, walk tall and carry a big stick." They were not referring to the Christian philosophy. I believe when a Christian presses toward the goal he will be able to withstand temptation, but only if he is carrying a rod. My rod of authority was the Word of God, and I was learning to wield it with love.

"My dear child..." I said with a gentleness that only comes from experience. "The pontiff you are approaching is under a different master. He is under the control of the Godhead, Jesus Christ himself. What we all need is a teacher who can address to us the basics of love. Then we apply love in the world in which we live." I looked over at Earnestine, who was humbly praying for my meeting with the Patriarch. I could see it in her eyes and looked forward to Irina. "I don't know if you have ever been introduced to Jesus, but He came to give love and to encourage life and freedom. Everything else is from the thesaurus of the evil one."

Her smile faded. She was being convicted by the Holy Spirit. My words were like seed planted on good ground.

"Irina," I said. "God is in control of life. She digested my words. We were at the Patriarch Cathedral, and it was beautiful, with several gold-painted domes. As we arrived, the limo pulled up in front of the cathedral for our appointment and Irina began to tell us some history on the Cathedral.

Chapter 7

Patriarch Alexis VIP Section

By the time we exited the limousine at the side steps to the cathedral, Earnestine and Irina were scrambling to get our video and still camera. The arrangement was to enter through a special VIP entrance and sit in a special VIP section.

Irina's English was impeccable, except when she had to stop if there was American slang incorporated into the conversation. The expressive eyes revealed much more about her thoughts than her speech. As we stepped through the ornately-carved doors into the side entrance of the Patriarch's Cathedral, the sight was awesome. The beautiful frescos and mountings on the ceiling reminded me of the movie classic, *Quo Vadis*. I'd heard stories about the grandeur, but it far exceeded the beauty I had envisioned, more than I ever imagined. Irina, who had lived in Russia most of her life as an avowed atheist, felt the awesomeness and expressed it openly. I felt the impact on my spirit, too, seeing the storehouse of jewels, gems, and wealth.

"Oh, Chris, it's so... lovely," said Earnestine, almost in a prayer-like whisper. Her amber hair looked brighter in the light. I could have sworn her eyes were a deeper hue of hazel as she reached out to touch the huge columns of marble. I touched the columns that appeared to support the ornately decorated the columns that appeared to support the ornately decorated porticos like layers of crinolines under a velvet dress. At intervals the columns seemed to be supporting nothing, save the ornately-carved boards across the top. It took great workmanship to construct such a cathedral. Each facet was intricately designed. Every Orthodox church in Russia has icons, and this one seemed to be designed to blaze from the wall.

As a child, I was an altar boy in the Orthodox church. The moment I stepped inside the cathedral it hit me, the memories attached but buried deep in the recesses of time. With those memories came a bolt of recollection that no woman is ever allowed behind the altar in the Holy of Holies.

"Oh, Earnestine I can't believe I could have forgotten such an important law. No woman is allowed inside the Holy of Holies. I'll have to find someone else to work the camera." I tried my best to explain and clarify the rules to Irina and Earnestine.

The Archbishop came out to greet me and invited me behind the altar. As I walked toward the altar, I pondered in my heart who will run the video and take pictures. I asked the Archbishop if one of the priests behind the altar help me. He responded with a hearty "*Kala* (yes)" in Greek. We will get you a special assistant."

I entered behind the altar and was amazed to see seventy-five priests. The Archbishop said, "Here is Father Vladimir. He will help you create the video."

Father Vladimir eagerly stepped forward. The way he handled the camera, I knew he was a natural.

It sounded like a voice from heaven. "Oh, I appreciate that," I said humbly. "I seldom hear Greek spoken." I kissed his hand. It was expected. It opened his spirit to me, and we struck it off well. We had a lot to talk about while waiting for the Patriarch to finish the service. Once the first service was over, the Patriarch turned to undress his vestment. It was quickly put away.

The Patriarch stood before me. I smiled and kissed his hand and wished him well. I couldn't help but notice the eyes. The looked tired, but very kind. There was immediate rapport. I thought of the huge responsibility he carried on his shoulders.

"God has sent me here to renew the minds of the people of Russia. They know Him in the head, but they need Jesus Christ in the heart," I said, using hand gestures, trying very hard to get my message over.

He listened attentively. I told him of one of my meetings with Patriarch Athenagoras when he was alive, remembering and sharing the words Athenagoras had used in reference to me. He told me, "I do not know what to do with you, Chris Panos. I can't make you a Bishop because you are married, and I can't make you a priest; they would crucify you.

"You are an Apostolos in Greek (an apostle), a sent one," he said, "called to the nations. You must remain a businessman, then they cannot harm you."

Turning to the Patriarch, I offered this testimony: "I would like to hold a crusade in Red Square. We could build a platform, and I could preach Christ. We could renew their spirit. I want them to get Jesus from their mind down into their heart." I gestured again with my hands.

The Patriarch smiled, but was silent, allowing me ample time to speak. As I continued, he was quite receptive, listening intently, taking it all in, giving an occasional nod in agreement. He allowed me time to say what I had come to say. I came to the part of my lawful vow. I proceeded to give the contract to the Church. The legal right to a percentage of royalties to my book, *God's Spy*.

When he discovered that I was finished, he smiled.

"Thank you, Mr. Panos. We can use this. I encourage you in your endeavors. Let's pray that God blesses this work." He talked for some time, but before he closed, he blessed the vow and said, "Amen."

"Boris Yeltsin has given me a special invitation to come back," I said at the finish of our conversation.

He smiled richly. "And I invite you back, too," he said, offering the words with great sincerity. "Come back and I will allow you to preach in all of my cathedrals." I left *God's Spy* in the Patriarch's hand as a witness of the miraculous. He thanked me and embraced me the traditional way.

I smiled to thank him graciously. I had been given the opportunity to meet with the Patriarch, and I had been engaged to preach and minister over radio and television all over Russia. What a miracle for this little Greek boy, a Bible smuggler from Galveston, Texas. At that moment in my life, I knew more than ever that God had hold of my life and was steering my course.

I had come home to my people, and to people who needed the message of salvation so badly.

Chapter 8

We Became Tourists

As a Christian, an American Christian, I knew I had freedom of worship that other people around the globe did not have. I reflected on the beauty of the onion-domed buildings, the sadness on the faces of her people, the emptiness in the hearts of people forever imprisoned. Disallowing belief in God and in allowing the exaltation of man above all else seemed to be a false analogy of the word. In my eyes they were people doubtful of love, and looking for it desperately. The disbelief in God has a way of becoming part of the personality. They truly have become people turned away, backslided from God.

"More than half a century has come and gone. The onion domes of the Orthodox churches remain the most striking structures dotting the horizons of our Russian cities," said the elderly gentlemen we met in the park the previous day. Having traveled extensively throughout Russia, I knew the travel brochures touted the same message, but this elderly man did not need a brochure to tell us of the beauty he saw. It was so breathtaking. Like looking at the seven wonders of the world, I stood looking up at their massive spires reaching upward, toward heaven. I likened them to upswept arms offering praises to an almighty God. The praises had to be in secret from fearful people controlled by the state. So intensely that it seemed the spires themselves had become their only means of expression to God.

Earnestine and I had been walking and exploring. Suddenly I caught sight of a familiar face. I guess I should say a familiar head.

A half-block away, half-hidden by a huge portico extending out from a building, I saw the bald head first. I had no idea how long we had been followed.

"Remember the man with the bald cantaloupe head I spoke to you about?" I said to Earnestine. "Well, don't look now, but he just took a snapshot of you and me."

"Do you think he is a friend or foe?"

"I think later I'll try and recruit him."

We slipped inside the massive doors to the cathedral, a timely gesture since it was only a few minutes before the service was to begin. A loyal parishioner took time to visit with us. I kept looking over our shoulder to see if we had been followed. We hadn't.

"It is always nice to see our visitors pausing and appreciating our beauty," said the happy-looking gentleman with the infectious smile.

"Tell us about your church service," said Earnestine, intent on hearing and touching the lifeblood of their service.

He smiled at Earnestine's request. "The Bishop or Patriarch dons a majestic robe known as the vestment. The Russian Orthodox liturgy was borrowed from the court ceremony of Byzantine emperors who regarded themselves as representatives of Christ on earth," he said very matter-of-factly, trying to set in our minds the reasoning behind such pageantry.

"A vestment is a beautiful piece of history," I added.

"It is supposed to reflect the very best of materials, of colors, and of what has been," said the elderly gentleman. Earnestine hung on every word, enraptured with his teaching. He had a compelling voice.

"There is something almost prayerful in the manner of dress which seems to create a tie between the Bishop and members. In the smaller cities, the churches and the Bishop have closer ties, receiving their guests at his residence. The parish priest and his family wait for their guests to share at a meal whatever is available. One man had a little piece of meat. He cut 12 little pieces so all 12 could have one piece of meat. They brought flowers and gave them one to another." He smiled. "We Russians appreciate beauty in life."

We listened, trying to glean the meaning of what he was saying.

"The vestment is created with some of the most beautiful Greek brocades and lush velvets available. The jewels are all securely attached with gold and silver thread." He seemed reflective, making gesture with his hands. "You will see many shades of turquoises which come from Persia."

"And the emeralds?"

"Emeralds are from our very own Ural Mountains." He was lost in his own thoughts as he explained further. "We do not have access to rubies; they are brought in from Burma in the Orient, but some of the most beautiful pearls come from the Crimea and Persian Gulf, which are much sought-after additions for the vestments."

"Who creates the vestments?" I asked as we continued trying to grasp the meaning of it all.

"The nuns of different orders are responsible for the vestments." He didn't pause. "The members of the congregation reverently stand throughout the service. The Patriarch will dress and commence the service, which might last three or four hours. From this he leads a grand procession through the nave and back to the altar, making his slow process through the church as a male choir sings hymns with such a harmonic sound. It was almost angel-like. After the ceremony occurs the reading of the Gospels."

I knew from the history books that so deep were the Russian's honor for the Scriptures that the Czars spent great fortunes having the sacred books bound. One jewel-studded book was overlaid in gold weighing 57 pounds.

The little gentleman smiled, offering Earnestine his genuine smile. "In the climax of the ceremony, the priest enters the sanctuary to bless the bread and wine which represent Christ's body and blood. This is called the Eucharist."

As a Greek Orthodox myself, I was seasoned about the religious affairs. I also knew that in the past, those that pursued following it were actively discouraged by the state. The individual churches were allowed to stand only if under direct leadership of the state. Those that attended were chastised for it, sometimes openly. The state had a way of ruling lives, but the Russian peoples from the earliest days to the present, were deeply moved by beauty in all forms. Possibly it was their only means of reaching perfection.

After getting to know the people, I was in wonder at some of their expressions. Through the innocence of a child, the style of love, or their music, they had a whole conditioning process to produce a perfect Russia. The effect on the simple was always the same. They stood with eyes cast down. The Communist Party allowed nothing less.

Out of the corner of my eye I saw a lone figure slip in through the large doors. It was becoming almost comical, the bald head bobbing in and out of places, hiding around corners. I'd spent twenty some years watching. I knew the spy-catching game front and back, from a street agent to the executive suite.

"The agency has a problem," said one of my brothers. I laughed when they told me this. Those in leadership said that the problem had a name: "Chris Panos." If I was their problem, I was not sorry. I was only doing what I was called to do. I had my assignment while doing what I was called to do.

Chapter 9

The Romanovs
(Grandmother Elena Romanov, Korniloff)

People often ask, "How did you get from the little port city of Galveston, Texas, to *God's Spy* and double agent?"

I laugh and say, "God miraculously intervened in my life."

The next question people ask has been a question I have asked myself over and over: "Why Russia? Aren't there enough places across the world dying for the Gospel?"

How do I answer that? In my short lifetime I have traveled around the world; I've been to China, India, the Baltic states, but over and over I kept returning to Russia. When I think of it now, it must have had something to do with my genetics and heritage. I think back to all the stories handed down by my family, and I am awed that so much of my past is still missing. But as a history buff, I'm finding that the tiny fragments I have gleaned from those close accounts are emerging as great landmarks to my past.

My Grandmother Elena Romanov Korniloff, and my grandfather, Petros Peters, lived during the very turbulent period of the 1860's. Life for Grandmother Elena Romanov Korniloff began at the Czar's Palace in St. Petersburg. Sometimes I sit and try to imagine what it might have been like growing up among royalty.

In 1913, the aristocrats were in their zenith. It was a very fashionable society, an elaborate time to be alive. Those who had money broadcast it. Those who had nothing were at the mercy of the very rich. But with every beginning, there must be an ending. Within five years, three European empires would be defeated, three emperors would die, others would flee into exile, and the ancient dynasties of the Habsburgs and Romanovs would crumble. Great changes were taking place, bringing about great changes in my family's life also.

The remainder of the story of the Czar's family is history. Mystery and contradiction surround the case. Volumes of original testimony, police reports, affidavits were all lost for decades to follow. Who knows just how accurate the stories are, but I remember accounts handed down in my own family, stories shrouded in secrecy because of my family's intimate connection to the Romanov family.

The history of the Grandmother, Elena Romanov, later Elena Romanov Korniloff in life, was a miracle, like my own. She fled Russia into Greece with the tutor, Petros Peters, who took her to Constantinople where he entered one of the most noted religious schools of the world centered there. Just barely fifteen, Elena used the time wisely. It offered needed time for the problems to abate in Russia and for Elena to grow up. More importantly, it afforded the time for Petros to build himself the prestige needed to be worthy of her. A priest was the next highest calling a man could aspire to after nobility at that time. How else might he be able to ask for her hand in marriage?

.Elena Romanov Korniloff became Elena Romanov Korniloff Peters, and almost immediately a child was born to this union. There was another child, the last one being a girl and named Catherine, a fine Czarist name.

When the authorities in Russia heard about it, they sent an envoy accompanied by six royal guards to Greece. "We have come to retrieve our frail little Elena back to us." There was grave concern back in Russia for her health and safety.

"I am overjoyed to see you, but I cannot go back. I must stay here. This is my rightful place now," she said with great conviction. She opted to stay instead in Greece at a place much below her past level of aristocracy.

But her life was cut short. Grandmother Elena lived only long enough to bear Petros two sons and two daughters. She died not long after giving birth to Catherine. It was said that Petros grieved deeply over the death. He felt that if he had not brought her to Greece to such a harsh life, possibly she would still be alive. Who could say?

The sons, Jim and Tom Peters, grew strong and made their way to America via sailing ships. They had a dream to fulfill. Once they had some money set aside, they brought their sisters Dimitria and Catherine to America.

Grandfather Petros stayed behind to serve his God. Later he was also brought to America. In my discovery of information I find that he later became noted for taking the message of Jesus to the hamlets surrounding the city of Tripoli.

In a little port city in America, down on Galveston Island, Catherine stepped off of a sailing ship. She, too, had come to America seeking a dream. It wasn't an easy transition, but the area reminded her of her home in Greece.

Who was this daughter of Elena? Her full name was Catherine Romanov Korniloff Peters Panos. My mother, the Grand Niece to Alexander II, Czar of Russia. Over the years I have been asked many times why I've been so drawn to the struggles in Russia and have such a strong desire to smuggle Bibles into Russia when my very life was at risk. Possibly the unsolved stories from my own past pressed down on me. Maybe those accounts were the basic motivation for me to risk my life for people I was somehow attached to but never had the opportunity to know.

God visited me on that death bed, down in Galveston. He extended His outstretched hand to me, setting me aside to take the Good News of Christ to the world... God had a purpose for my life as He does for yours.

Chapter 10

Mamma & Pappa

Growing up down on Galveston Island during my impulsive years, I was a highly-charged, fast-paced little boy who was always finding his way into one jam after another. Looking back, I am convinced God had His hand on my life even then.

From a little guy my mamma called me a good boy. "What does than mean, Mamma?" I asked. I knew the difference between good and bad, and I couldn't say I agreed with her definition.

"You will wash those dishes till you learn how to control yourself," said Pappa with conviction.

As a child I played hard and laughed quickly, intent on being at the head of the class, but sometimes it was not through conventional methods. And I learned early that I was Greek, which meant I was different from most boys. They expected more from me, especially the priest when he told us about the Greek heroes.

"Who is the most famous Greek of all times?" he'd ask.

After about a thousand times I should have remembered, but I was a kid worrying about kid things, not dead heroes from years past. With all the Greek religion and Greek culture I was being trained to endure... wow, they were hard lessons to live sometimes. My father had moved us to Fort Worth, Texas and started a new restaurant called T & P Cafeteria. It was across from the main post office, and business was booming.

One day I was out looking for excitement. Finding none, I did what I did best. I invented some. I decided to visit the dime store near our house. Once I was inside, I walked around a table of toys. I passed by these particular items at least six times before I spied a new addition to their stock. I can attest that this store did an excellent job of merchandising, for it was from their artistic merchandising that I was introduced to the word "covet."

I walked around that big old store, and the desire for those tiny toy soldiers, each one poised to do battle, became an overpowering obsession for me. On my seventh trip around the table a brown paper bag appeared in my hand and the toy soldiers jumped in unnoticed. All I could think of was the hours of fun I could have later doing battle with them. I'd been in the five and dime store on many occasions, but that day I met the devil in disguise. But I think he and I had been acquainted for some time.

I must admit I felt pretty smug when I left the store that day with my prize tucked under my arm. "Look here, James," I said to my friend. "And there was not store detective following me or storekeeper chasing after me."

Two blocks away from the store I looked over to the park where I usually played. Suddenly I saw something. I rubbed my eyes, squinted, and looked again. It was a big Jesus Christ. Now, this wasn't a statue of Jesus, but it was a real live Jesus, and He was looking directly at me. I was so frightened I took off in a run.

"I have to get home," I said under my breath. I needed to get home; I needed to get away from whatever it was that I had seen in the park. The faster I ran, the more the image stayed in my mind. I couldn't forget those tears I'd seen streaming down his face. The wind cut at my lungs and I could hardly breathe. I knew the tears on His face were for me, for what He had seen me do. I saw flashed images as I ran through the streets. The main sight I recalled. It was the appearance of love on the face of Jesus as He called me.

It is impossible for me to remember the past without speaking of this visit from Jesus. Jesus cared enough to appear to this little boy and to admonish him. Suddenly I was sure that if He cared this much for me, He cared that much for the whole world.

"Please forgive me," I begged, as I ran through the streets bouncing off the shrubbery and buildings. "I promise I will never make you cry again," I cried through my childish tears.

Over the years in the little Greek community in Fort Worth, Texas, I forgot that event and my miracle birth. At that moment I had a flashback to the past when the Lord appeared to my mother and said, "Even though you have named the child Petros, I want you to change his name to Christos, for he will suffer as I suffered." My mother could see the Lord Jesus Christ in the ceiling fan with the thorns pressed against his brow. "Do not be afraid; Christos will not die, but he will live."

It was at that time that Dr. Cook at John Sealey Hospital took a hose and put it into my mouth. The doctor sucked the mucous from my body. Then he turned me over and slapped me on the rear end. Then life was infused into my body. George Panos witnessed this complete miracle and has stated over the years, "Christos started kicking and he is still kicking today."

Growing up and moving to Houston, Texas, with my family was such a joy. It seemed as though a great burden was behind me. Thank God Fort Worth is in the past, and little did I know that I would be meeting the lady that would change my life. I met my wife, Earnestine, and I fell madly in love with her and we got married. It is strange that my name is Christos, and Christos means born after Christ in the Greek and Earnestine's name in the Greek means resurrection. One warm night in a duplex apartment we had rented on Clay Street in Houston, Texas, the Lord appeared to Earnestine in a dream. She suddenly also came face to face with the Savior, and she witnessed Jesus coming in the clouds to rapture the church and she cried out, "Please Lord, don't come now, I'm not ready." Earnestine frantically cried out, "Chris, wake up. I just saw the Lord coming back in the clouds to take his church to heaven."

I rolled over and said, "Earnestine, please go back to sleep." Earnestine realized I did not understand and she rolled over and pondered in her heart the majestic scene that she had just witnessed in her dream.

I told her later, "If that is what you want to believe in, it's okay with me. Earnestine, please understand. I really don't know what you are talking about. My grandfather was a priest and I belong to the Greek Orthodox family church. I don't know what you are talking about." Down deep in my heart I felt well that my wife was reaching out to God. I guess you might say that the fear of the Lord had captured my heart, and I always felt uneasy when religion was mentioned to me.

I was the son of a chef and the grandson of a priest of the Greek Orthodox church, and we were very close. We were raised to respect and depend upon each another. Sunday was the only day our cafe was closed. The older I got, the more I looked forward to Sunday, not because I was so religious, but I worked alongside my parents in their restaurant and it was my only free time. I made a deduction real soon, though. No matter how hard we seemed to work, money was something that passed through our hands. Very little of the green stuff seems destined to stay around, which drove me to perfection. I desperately wanted and needed to become a millionaire. Who wanted to live their life and end up penniless? I needed to be looked up to, and I wanted the recognition.

My father made a decent living, but I was smarter than him, or so I thought. It was "just a matter of timing," I thought. With my wit and enough perseverance, coupled with my good business sense, I should be able to fling into the millionaire bracket quickly. As you can see, I had no ego. When it didn't happen overnight, I was highly discouraged.

"What have you been doing with yourself?" asked an acquaintance I had not seen for years.

"Still working on that million," I tossed back. I thought back on the array of my past business adventures. One new adventure after another seemed to fall into my lap. I'd soon conquer it and be off looking for another. I tried my hand at the restaurant business. Then it was boots and shoes. I even tried the shoeshine business and I became a success at them all. I learned each business quickly, mastered it, then grew quickly tired of it, feeling I needed to move onto something bigger and better.

Those who knew me said I was born with keen business sense. I was capable of remembering facts and numbers like a computer. I had a lot of salesmanship, too, and I finally edged myself into the real estate and building business. Don't take me wrong when I tell you this, but within myself, I was a well-polished Greek, unattached to the Lord. I was not about to give credit for my successes to anyone other than me. In my haughty spirit I knew that whatever I laid my hand to, it would ultimately become a success, and I wasn't ashamed to tell anyone that I had what it took to make things happen. And things were happening.

As a spiffy dresser, I loved expensive clothes. I guess you could say it was part of my character to envy men who drove Rolls Royces. If that wasn't enough to finish off my character, I liked to flash money and show off my rings. Of course none of this was a secret to anyone who knew me. I began to accumulate stocks and bonds and real estate properties, along with luxurious material possessions. With it came the sin, black as ebony. Drinking and smoking and of course gambling, all part of an exalted life.

"You drink too much, Chris Panos," said an unwelcome acquaintance. I knew I drank too much and hustled too much, too. Social drinks now and then might not upset the business and moral senses, but if it becomes a part of everyday routine, it takes its toll.

The business corporations I set up became my empire. To protect them, then, became my number one goal in life. My business sense set me ahead of the rest. I was confident and self-sufficient. Who did I need beyond myself? God must have thought differently. I think Earnestine was beginning to wonder what she needed me for.

Chapter 11

My Eye Was Laying on My Cheek

Houston, Texas, was big even back in the thirties and forties. Big enough to get lost in or find your true love. I accomplished both.

My love affair was a whirlwind courtship. I took Earnestine everywhere. We were a twosome, and from that very first thirty-day anniversary, I pleaded, "Earnestine, please marry me."

"Chris Panos, I'm not ready to get married. We're too young," she'd say every time I asked.

I began to propose to her daily. It must have finally worn her down. She married me, even in the darkness of my sin, and we started off our life together.

When two people start off a relationship, neither knows what the future holds, nor what the other person is really like. Years later, still looking to fill an empty hole in my soul, I drank more and gambled more. I had an unnatural craving for money. Earnestine was feeling guilty about her life separated from God and began to seek the God of her childhood. By a miracle she found him, but it didn't help us. It actually made things worse. Instead of healing our marriage, it began to tear us apart. She was growing to hate what she saw happening with me. I felt about the same about her newfound religion.

"I don't care what you do, Earnestine. Just don't ask anything of me. I'm perfectly happy doing just what I am doing."

Earnestine kept her thoughts to herself, but she did continue to pray for me and reach out to an affectionate God. I could see these changes and I found them threatening. This God seemed to be more important to her than I was.

One evening, angry over Earnestine's newfound friends and her attraction to this man called Jesus, I fled the house for another drinking binge.

"I don't care what you're doing with your life, just leave me out of it," I said as I slammed out the door. I hated everything that stepped into my path that mirrored what I knew I needed to be, or even hoped to be. I could remedy that. I took it upon myself to dispense my own prescription: more booze.

I looked good and smelled good. It was a combination of expensive cologne and denatured alcohol. To get away from all that was obviously bothering me, I decided to stop off at another party. I liked those parties and fit right in.

On the way home I was well-inebriated and feeling dynamic. I had my contracting buddy along with me. I maneuvered my white Bonneville through the curves in the road, even straightened out a few in the process as I lay that Pontiac down close to the ground. We laughed boisterously, and I felt extremely courageous. The lines in the road were whizzing by at breakneck speed, but I felt confidant. I was an experienced driver and I was used to partying all night. I definitely wasn't ready to call it a night.

"Slow down, Chris," he screamed when the tires dropped off the edge of the road. "You're going to kill us both!"

He had entreated me earlier to allow him to drive when we left the party, but I wouldn't hear of it. I could handle a little alcohol. Actually I knew I'd consumed a lot, but I had driven in such stupors before.

Suddenly out of nowhere I lost control of the vehicle. The car left the pavement and careened off into the bar ditch, uprooting a tree in its path. I heard the horrible splintering crack as the car ran right through the huge tree, snapping it like a toothpick. We carried it thirty feet or so.

I'll never forget the deafening sounds: the screeching of tires, the screams of the man in the car with me... or was it my own? I heard an explosion and the breaking of glass, and a horrible loud scrapping of metal, then intense pain.

found myself anxious and excited about the opportunity to preach against the darkness, even though I had no idea how God was going to bring that opportunity about.

A few months later the opportunity did arise, and I knew in my heart God had been instrumental in bringing it to me. My interpreter, a staunch Christian, told me, "This pastor is a compromiser of the worst sort. He will have no hesitation in reporting you to the authorities if you chance to preach on forbidden subjects."

"Don't worry," I told him. "It will all work out. God is on our side." God would not have opened the door if I was going to have to stand with a gag in my mouth.

The Sunday morning I was scheduled to preach was cold and snowing. I trudged through snow and ice up to my kneecaps. It was blustery, too, but my heart was warm. It is no understatement to say I was emotionally charged. My interpreter and I arrived at the little church to find it jammed to the brim with young people. The pastor, however, was nowhere in sight. As we made our way to the front of the church, a young man hurried up to meet us.

"Hello," he said warmly. He spoke in Polish, and my interpreter related it all to me. "You must be Brother Panos."

"That's right," I told him.

"I am Boris Cherbanov, the assistant pastor here," he said excitedly. "Our pastor was called out of town suddenly and is unable to be here. He sends his regards. He asked me to tell you that he is very disappointed." Something about his face matched his actions. "We have a youth convention going on here right now. Young people from all of Poland are here in church this morning!"

"Wonderful," I replied. It was another benchmark. I couldn't wait to see what was about to unfold next. I was assured that somehow whatever I preached that morning would be carried out all over Poland to the many far-flung homes.

"What would you like me to preach on this morning?" I asked hesitantly, looking him directly in the eye.

"Didn't Pastor give you instructions?" he asked, clearing his throat.

"Yes, he did," I hedged. "But you are running the service now. I thought possibly I should check with you. Is your taste in sermons identical to his?"

"No, as a matter of fact not, but I must warn you that it will not be safe to preach what you would like. With a nationwide meeting like this, there will undoubtedly be several party spies planted in the audience."

I couldn't believe my ears. This young assistant pastor was sharing this with me... and yes, that was probably the understatement of the year. I knew that the Communist spies and the KGB were present in almost every church service behind the Iron Curtain. Additional spies were charged with the task of checking up on every foreign tourist, and still more agents were charged with protecting the politics of the Polish youth from anti-Communist influences. If there weren't spies in this church this morning, it would be an outright miracle.

I spotted the spies the second I mounted the platform. On the third row sat two young Russian men who were dressed immaculately. Behind the Iron Curtain it had never been difficult to spot a spy. I had a sixth sense, an inner presence of innate knowledge that relayed danger to me. I knew as well as I knew my own name they were spies. Often I would be able to detect even which country the person hailed from.

As soon as I saw the spies, all sorts of thoughts raced through my mind: *You can't preach salvation... they will arrest you. They will lock you up and toss away the key. They might even assassinate you.* I wondered if these thoughts could be detected by the audience. *Then they will probably beat you and torture you, and let's see you praise God then!*

All of these thoughts were natural tricks of the devil. He uses them to attack us at the most vulnerable moment. Need I relate the vulnerable state I felt pressed into? No matter how many times I flew in and out of great risk areas, even as I would manage to escape, it carried with it a great measure of fear. My knees were shaking that morning.

The fear traveled from the top of my head to the bottom of my toes. It was more than a high imagination now. It was an out-and-out attack by satanic forces thinking they could halt my ability to preach the Gospel to this needy youth of Poland.

I was the only one in the room that spoke English other than the interpreter, but I wasn't foolish. If something went wrong, it wouldn't be the assistant pastor or even the interpreter who would be dragged off, beaten, and thrown in prison. It would be me, and it placed a heavy weight on my shoulders.

Suddenly I looked out across the crowd of beautiful and youthful faces waiting for a message that had the power to change their life. I thought of my ancestors who had fought the elements and walked the snow-covered ground of Russia. Even though I had never known them, I thought of my ancestors who lay buried in anonymity, never having known the saving grace of my Lord Jesus, and I wept in my soul.

Suddenly, as I stepped forward, I had a smile for the young crowd. "If God is for me, who can be against me? Greater is He that is in me than he that is in the world. God has not given me the spirit of fear. Jesus will never leave me nor forsake me. No weapon that is formed against me will prosper." I spoke quietly. I repeated every verse of Scripture that came to mind, and continued to quote Scriptures as the interpreter made my introduction. When he finally pronounced my name, he handed me the microphone and walked over to the sidelines to translate.

Stepping forward, my breath caught in my throat, but I launched into the hardest-hitting sermon I had ever preached. I quoted Scripture after Scripture on the Blood and the Atonement, and on the Cross, and of Christ crucified and risen. That's when I began to smile. "He is risen," I said with conviction. Jesus had risen and was now sitting on the right hand of God. He made it possible for me to come to far-away places to share His perfect plan of salvation. A wave of assurance passed over me.

Phrase upon phrase, I delivered the message God gave. My interpreter was translating enthusiastically. Suddenly one of the assumed spies jumped to his feet and came running toward the front of the church. I thought he was coming forward to kill me or stop the sermon. He didn't. Instead he dropped to his knees and began to weep. He wept as though he was marching through a literal burning hell. Minutes later the other spy jumped up and ran to the altar. Glitches of thoughts were flashing through my mind. I suspected these actions were just some facades to catch me. They are here to disrupt the service. *You will see soon*, said a voice inside my head. Even as I stood continuing to preach, I watched the grown men. The moment they really began to weep, I knew that God had touched them, just as He had touched a hardened Chris Panos years earlier when he was headed down the road to hell.

Minutes after the invitation, the front of the church was filled to capacity with young Polish students. They came weeping for a life my sermon had laid bare before them. Most were seeking answers to emotional and spiritual needs. I have traveled the world. People may come from different cultures and stations in life, but even if a human being has been taught since birth that there is no God, the necessity to believe is implanted there. The vacancy inside the human heart is the same, whether poor and lowly or high and prideful. All are sinful souls, and the need is equally great for all. God meets us individually. The same God who flung the stars across the galaxies, breathed the breath of life into a tiny child. He cares—for you, and me, and even a KGB agent.

Chapter 13

We Came to Spy on You

After the service was over, the two spies stood waiting to talk to me. I had so many converts wanting to shake my hand and ask questions, it took much longer than expected. I praised God for the outpouring of His Spirit, and I felt greatly humbled to think that possibly one of these beautiful youth might one day be following in my steps—smuggling Bibles and sharing the Gospel for the Lord.

I shook the last hand and turned to face the two KGB agents who had waited so patiently.

"We have a confession to make," said the shorter of the two. "We came to spy on you, Mr. Panos, to find a way to put a stop to your foolish preaching."

"I know," I said very quietly.

"If you happened to preach a sermon on salvation, we had orders to report you immediately."

"I know," I said again. "The Holy Spirit told me that was why you were here."

"Then why did you preach it?" they asked with surprise, almost in unison. "Many times they send other spies, ones we do not know about, to see if our reports agree."

"I have to preach what God has called me to preach," I said. "And no, there were no others this time," I said assuredly.

"How do you know?"

"If so, God would have pointed them out to me, just as he pointed out the two of you." I lay my hand on their shoulders.

"Of course, we will not report you now," they added.

"I know," I said again. "God has changed you. Where Jesus enters, God's Spirit enters.

The two KGB agents would not let me walk away. They had questions, real and genuine questions. Even in America where the philosophy of belief in God resounds from the very core of our freedom, some people have a hard time with the idea of a power beyond their own selves. But at the same time, we are fortunate. People given the freedom of choice have been blessed both spiritually and financially. We have a shelter over our heads and food for our stomachs. But still the buildings beckon us to a more intimate walk with a Holy God.

"Where do we go from here?" they asked with great sincerity.

"God will direct you." I handed them each a Bible. "Read this. Every page. It's the recorded words of a Holy God, and it was written to you personally. Think about that! A Holy God, out in the expanses of our universe, who knows everything there is to know, is there for you. In your future unguarded moments, when you need answers to questions, He will be there to talk you, personally, through His Word as He did to all mankind before you. As He did to me tonight when He told me who you were and why you were here."

They took the Bibles, the object of their search for a lifetime. Now they were searching for a different cause, like Paul after his Damascus experience. Now they were here asking about Him and wanting to know more about Him.

"You were bought with a price," I said turning to admonish each one. I wanted desperately to impress this point. "You are a blood-bought possession of Jesus now, not the KGB's."

"The KGB could have us put to death over this treason."

"They might try. John 10:20 says, "But Satan, knowing that he is unable to pluck us out of our Father's hand, endeavors to do the next best thing to get us to jump out!"

They looked fearful.

"It won't be easy. I've heard stories about how hard it is to get away from the KGB." Suddenly my heart went out to them. "Pray and seek His will for your life. It will come to you like the manna sent from heaven like to the children of Israel, one day at a time." I laid my hands on the two young men and prayed God's blessing on them that day, for their future, for their abiding faith, and I rebuked the demons that hovered over the freedomless land. I felt the very presence of them hovering over these two men, and I prayed for God to loose the powers that had controlled them in the past.

As for me, I did not understand all that was going on either, but I did know one thing. God is unfathomable. Like the mighty oceans that can touch all the shores at once. The Holy Spirit pours His mercy on a gathering of strangers, whether dressed in Arab garb, a Sari from India, or even an olive green military uniform of a Russian soldier. And after this meeting, I could attest to the fact that He could even touch a man wearing the attire of a Russian KGB agent.

Chapter 14

Masquerading As a Tourist

I couldn't remember how many trips I had made into Russia, but here I was flying toward Moscow doing something I did so well: masquerading as a tourist.

My original visa had been stamped to capacity, with some extensions added. When there was no more room to allow and entry to another nation, they issued me a new one. Before it was full, I lost that one. Now here I sat holding the third issued document and talking to the young man sitting next to me on the plane, sharing a few moments of conversation. I noted that the man was only vaguely responsive, but God stirred my spirit to talk to him anyway. Over the years, in my ministry, at times I would have a direct impression to remain quiet. Other times, even when I knew the person I was talking with was probably a KGB Operative, I would be instructed to share intimate things. I learned to depend on God's direction.

The young man continued to talk becoming a little more than mildly curious about me and my profession. After a few more minutes of conversation he introduced himself and asked a string of personal questions. He was a far cry from a friend, but his spirit did not threaten me.

"Do you smuggle Bibles?" he asked pointedly.

I noticed the eyes, so penetrating. The eyes were not beginning to bother me.

"Is it dull?" he asked with lifted brows.

He appeared void of something logical to say. I assumed he was from the party, one of those cursed by the simple people because he produced nothing and always wanted to be in the limelight. I had not told him I smuggled Bibles.

I laughed out loud. "Dull? Not if you consider being chased through the streets in the middle of the night or detained at customs for hours until they go through every piece of your baggage dull." I paused, wondering if it was a trap. "I've had it all happen once, or twice... at least."

He didn't smile. Instead he nodded a quick dismissal and turned his face to the window. What could I say? He sounded like he was green behind the ears, or he was plying me.

I looked around the plane. Two rows ahead and to the right I saw the shiny bald head. There was an uneasiness that swept over me when he turned in his seat. I remembered the call from a Mr. Frank from New York. I had kept the information from Earnestine. "I will explain it all the next time I see you," he'd said. "But for now, be watchful. There is someone following you. If you have not noticed, he is slightly built, maybe 135 pounds, rather nondescript except for a shiny, bald head."

Before the flight was over, the young gentleman sitting next to me posed many superficial questions. I could see the obsequiousness of his profession rewarded by privilege. His clothing spoke of special treatment when he withdrew it to show me a picture of his fiancée, something strange for a bonafide KGB operative. Either the new forces of agents were of a higher class, or they were being rewarded for their friendliness.

The man was definitely traveling first class. I would have placed him in the mid-strata of the established pyramid. After this there was the title, a really Communist directive, and finally the blissful state prophesied by Karl Marx.

I tired of the young man's questions and turned to face the window myself, while carefully keeping a check on the man two rows ahead. I had no clue to his identity.

As if a hint, the young party man stared over at the book jutting out of my attaché case. "So, are you a businessman?"

I cleared my throat. "Yes, and a teacher."

He repositioned himself in his seat. I thought he was going to say something, but he decided against it.

"God opens many doors for me," I said with a smile.

"Do those doors ever get slammed in your face?"

"When God opens a door, no man or principality or ruler of this dark world can alter His plan."

After my remark he folded his arms, leaned his head toward the isle and went to sleep, a nap that lasted hours. After having been hailed and sought-after for years as an excellent speaker, I smiled, wondering why he was so adverse to my words.

Resting back against my seat, I began thinking how God has been pressing me to reach the youth of Russia. It was close to two years now. Money had been painstakingly set aside to cover expenses. The account had grown, and here I was finally making my maiden voyage to put the idea to the test. I was praying for contacts to help make it a reality.

When the children of Israel were sent to the wilderness, God provided the manna. It was just enough for necessity, nothing more, just enough to keep them coming back to His well to get them through each day. God seemed to be keeping me close to him for the same reason.

I felt a tremendous burden for the young people of Russia, but my heart was battering me with a recurring question: What did I know about young people? I wasn't even sure of my ability to talk with them. I had a couple children of my own, but they were not teenagers, and besides, my title was Bible Smuggler, not Youth Leader. After much prayer, I decided Moscow University would be as good a place as any to begin my outreach.

The moment our flight landed, my infamous party man disappeared. So did the bald-headed man. All I saw were the customs agents as they herded us toward a bugged waiting room. I had been on the road too many years not to recognize the event. And as if this maneuver wasn't subtle enough, we watched as our luggage was taken from the plane and wheeled into a separate holding area. I sat waiting, assuming it would take a while. It did. Four hours. When the guards returned, they were dragging a trail of luggage behind them. They weren't happy. One of the guards approached me. I knew a miracle had already taken place. Before the trip, I had placed Gospels and New Testaments on top in my suitcase, above the rest of the items. By God's miracle, the bags had passed inspection. I claimed the bags and was rejoicing about another close escape and walking away. Suddenly one ugly, nails-for-breakfast agent approached me. I'm not exaggerating to say he was one of the biggest, ugliest Russian men I had ever laid eyes on. For a silent moment he stared me down.

"Open up that bag," he said, pointing to the larger of my two suitcases.

"In the Name of Jesus, I command you. Do not touch my bags." My voice was louder than normal and dispensed with authority, so much so that it even shocked me. Usually I voiced such things quietly under my breath or silently to myself, but this time I felt impressed to do otherwise.

The agent blinked. Either he did not hear my words or he did not understand them. For a fraction of a second he stood looking at me. He raised his hand like he might strike me. I didn't flinch. Something caught and stayed his hand.

"You've waited long enough," he said gruffly. "Pass on through."

I picked up my bags and walked on down the long corridor. I glanced back over my shoulder to see the big, gruff guard joining the crowd. In a boisterous voice he screamed out a command that shook me in my boots.

"How many of you came in on that airplane?" he screamed, motioning toward the Russian Aeroflot jet the group had just arrived on. Many raised their hands. "I'll take you over here." He motioned for them to form a line. "File by. I will check your bags."

I thanked God for His intervention for me and hurried on from the area.

Chapter 15

It's Great to Hear a Greek Voice

I left the airport in a run. I decided I'd stay at the Metropole, one of the nicer hotels. The word "nicer" is a deceptive word when one discusses accommodations in Russia, or most foreign countries for that matter. Few foreign motels are up to American standards.

I had been fasting and praying, something I did when I had special needs. As usual, my hunger pangs vanished after the first forty-eight hours. With the hardest part behind me, my plan was to continue fasting on an indefinite basis. God had other plans.

I went to my room and unloaded my luggage. No sooner was I in my room than I felt impressed to go down to the dining room. I couldn't understand it. If you have never submitted your body to fasting, you cannot comprehend the transformation that takes place. The body reached a point that it has no real need for food, and in my mind, it had not been long enough for my answer. But I obeyed.

The dining room was lighted and full to capacity of people busily talking. My eyes traveled the room looking for an empty table. Over in the far corner I saw one. Assuming it was the place for me, I threaded my way between the closely aligned furnishings and maneuvered around arms and legs protruding out in aisles. Overhead was a beautiful chandelier. I sat and waited to be served. The smoke was thick as fog. The tables were chock full of people drinking champagne. Suddenly, as if an amplifier had been attached to my ear, in addition to the buzz of intelligible Russian voices, I was overhearing snatches of understandable conversation.

"Greek!" I said out loud and turned to see who was speaking. At the table right next to me two young Greek girls and two Greek boys, all in their early twenties, were holding a spirited conversation.

"*Tikanis*," I said, greeting them.

"*Tikanis*," they responded, looking somewhat puzzled.

I stood to my feet and introduced myself as I moved closer to their table. I was extremely happy just to hear a familiar sound in the buzzing crowd.

"Sit, sit!" they said in unison. "It's great to hear another Greek," they said. Their smiles were genuine. "Have you eaten? Come eat with us," said the young man to the right of me.

They were eating pastries stuffed with spiced meat, accompanied by red cabbage and a salad of sliced tomatoes.

When the waiter arrived, I asked for the same. "Bring me a bowl of soup, too," I added, remembering how delicious the Russian Solanska soup was. The young man, Nicholas, who had curly black hair and dark beaded eyes, smiled and wiped his mouth. "This is Georgia." He pointed to the black-headed young lady sitting across the table. She was a knockout, blowing streams of smoke into the air. Her black hair and brown eyes sparkled like diamonds. "And this is CEO." He added pointing to the other girl. She was intelligent looking. "We're all enrolled at the Moscow University." Pedro, the other young man, was very quiet and listened intently. He was from Tripolis, Greece.

CEO had a nice smile. Perhaps they were the contacts I had been praying for? We chatted back and forth over our food, getting acquainted. Their smiles were receptive. They obviously had an interest in who I was and why I was in their city. Nicholas was the spokesperson.

"What are you doing in Russia, Mr. Panos?"

What should I say? After a brief moment I smiled and looked directly at them. "I smuggle Bibles into Russia." Almost as a dual action, the moment I offered my confession, I slapped a small Russian New Testament Bible on the marble tabletop.

The three students jerked as though I had deposited a snake in front on them instead of the Holy Scriptures. I guess they weren't used to talking to anyone quite so open.

"Please, be careful!" they chorused, speaking nearly in unison and under their breath. Their eyes scanned the room. "There are spies everywhere, and they watch very closely."

Nicholas looked like he could handle himself. He was a stout young man with massive shoulders and big hands. I tried to imagine what his hand would look like clenched into a fist.

"Don't worry," I said, looking at them. "My God is able to take care of me." Their eyes grew big. "I just came through customs with my bags full of Bibles."

"Well, it must have been a mistake on the agent's part," Georgia said to catch her breath.

"No, it was a miracle." I looked around the dining hall and back. "I was the only one on the plane whose luggage was not searched."

The statement was met with a hushed silence.

"We believe in God, too," said Nicholas, keeping his voice low. "We are Greek Orthodox." With raised brows and a low whistle, he added, "But if I tried such a thing as that, I am certain I would be arrested. What would make you think you could do such a thing?"

"I can be bold because I know God is with me," I said. I watched the questionable expression on each of their faces. "Just as God can be with you, too."

The three students looked at each other in disbelief.

I thought of the many times the Lord had covered me with his grace and blinded the eyes of customs agents. "As Greek Orthodox, you already know the way to God, because the Orthodox churches preach the Gospel. But it is not enough just to hear the Gospel; you need a personal relationship with the man called Jesus."

Their receptive minds tried to grasp what I was saying.

"If you really believe and act on that, God will hear your request." The words were piercing to the center of their doubts, to the center of their intelligence, the area where humans divide and part company with God.

"How do we do that?" Nicholas asked skeptically.

"You accept Jesus as Savior, as the one sent by God. And believe it as much as I believe He is going to take care of me when I pass through customs with my Bibles.

They were digesting my statement.

"Would you like to have that kind of assurance?" I asked. The girls looked.

"We would like to have such assurance," they told me.

Right there, sitting in that crowded dining room of the elegant Metropole Hotel, three Greek students became new babes in Christ. And I knew these three young people had been my appointed contacts.

Chapter 16

Communist Propaganda

Within a day, the three young Greek Orthodox students had become my couriers, smuggling Bibles into Moscow University and distributing them to the other students. I had worried about finding contacts. How beautifully God had worked it all out. In Moscow, a city of six million people, God led me to the right restaurant, at the right hotel; in that enormously crowded dining hall he helped me find a seat less than two feet away from the table at which my prayed for contacts were sitting. God made it happen. What a coincidence.

God manifested himself to those young people, and in a few days the three new converts became my most zealous evangelists.

It seemed to be my trip for encounters in restaurants. Just a few days after I met the Greek students, I entered the Metropole dining room again. This time it was not so crowded. I found an empty table right away and sat down. In Moscow it is the custom that the first person to sit at a table has the authority to give permission for others to sit. As the restaurant filled, an English couple arrived.

"Would you mind if we sat with you?" they asked as they searched for a place to sit.

"Please do," I said, smiling as I moved my plate over allowing them more room to sit. British to the core, they ordered tea which arrived in little glasses encased in silver holders. With it came several kinds of pastry. I observed the events taking place. Soon after the serving of tea, a Russian lady came up.

"May I sit with you?" she asked in broken English.

"Please do," we told her. I was busy with my lunch, so I didn't take time to investigate our newest addition to the table.

She was short and vivacious. "I teach a class of six-year-olds," she informed us immediately, as soon as she was seated. She didn't give us a chance to warm up to her before she proceeded, "I tell them of our great father Lenin."

I continued to eat my meal. She rattled on, spouting a great deal of Communist propaganda about what a great deliverer Lenin was and how he had delivered Russia from capitalism and from the Czar.

"He gave the Russian people real freedom," she said, trying hard to get a response.

The longer she spoke, the more difficult it was for me to remain passive. I knew, in my spirit, that she was a KGB bloodhound. I didn't have proof. I guess she just fit the description I had conceived in my mind after years of dealing with the KGB. Finally she paused long enough to take a breath.

"My dear lady," I said kindly, trying to use tact and gentleness. "Lenin was not the deliverer. Jesus Christ was sent to deliver all mankind, whether Greek, Jews, Englishman, or Russian." I tried to speak in the gentleness of spirit, knowing the delicate a subject I was broaching.

"What do you do?" she asked, through narrowed eyes.

"You are a teacher. I also am a teacher," I said, looking for the right words to use. "I teach that 'God so loved the world He gave His only begotten Son that whosoever believeth in Him, should not perish, but have everlasting life.' In my heart, kind lady, I am assured through God's Word that in Him is the only true freedom we will ever find in this life."

She sat intently surveying me, unsure on how to respond. After careful consideration, she jumped from her chair and stomped her foot. "Lenin is the only deliverer!" If I could read her mind, she had more to report but decided against it. She wheeled around on her heels and stalked off through the crowd. I prayed for her as she strode off. The rest of us sat in stunned silence as the staccato of her heels receded into the background. I looked up. The English woman on my right was very quiet. I wasn't sure if she was upset at what I had said or at the lady's response. Suddenly, while swallowing back tears that were filling her eyes, and in spite of her struggling against it, she spilled outward her feelings.

"If you love this Jesus enough to risk everything to tell his story here in Russia, I am humbled. I wish I could say my life had such meaning." She faltered, looking over to her partner, then away. "I'm not sure I care enough about anyone to be able to do that."

"It is because I believe in Him," I said quietly. "He cared enough for me." My words seemed to hang, waiting a response. The man sat stiff-backed. She bowed her head. No words came.

"His blood can cleanse your heart, right now, even here," I said.

Coming as a welcome plea, her expression brightened. "I would like to believe in this man called Jesus," she said.

At that moment I so wanted Jesus to empower her with the same bold assurance I felt. In the following minutes He did visit the English lady, right there, in that very spot!

Not a bad score for one Russian restaurant: three Greek Orthodox students and an English schoolteacher, all in the same trip. Her partner looked on in stunned silence. I didn't think he was as adverse as much as shocked and wondering.

The excitement was not over yet. Several hours later I headed back toward my room there at the Metropole. Making my way back through the lobby, I stopped to admire the antique architecture. By American standards, the Metropole Hotel is not luxurious, although the lobby and the dining room retain an old-world flavor: high ceilings and a quaint elegance which appealed to me. But in the individual rooms, at least the rooms I could afford, the furnishings were drab and offered only small comforts.

I was exhausted and anxious for a good night's sleep. Each step I took, I lamented about the sleeping arrangements provided by the hotel Metropole. Not much more than a narrow cot, I murmured to myself. Imagine my surprise when I opened the door to my room, and there, sitting perched atop my bed, was a young and beautiful, half-clad lady. From the open doorway, I could see that she had little more on than a sort of slip or nightie.

"Lord, what should I do," I said in a whisper of a prayer.

"Tell her about me," the answer came.

"Young lady, who are you?" I called into the darkness. Her eyes said it all. "It is pretty obvious that you need something more than what I have to give." I waited a response but none came. "I know someone who can help you. His name is the name above all else. His name is the counselor. His name is Jesus." I spoke with authority, courageously, as I advanced a few steps into the room. Bible verses, pictures, and scenes from God's Words flashed through my mind. "He died, even for a woman like you," I said finally, as gently as I knew how. I don't remember all I said, but obviously God was speaking through me to her.

With a startled cry she jumped from the bed, grabbed for her things that had been hastily tossed to the floor, and ran off down the hall. I poked my head out into the hallway in hopes of seeing where she went. She had vanished into thin air. There hadn't been enough time to reach the elevator or the stairs. After careful investigation, I found out that the Russian Aeroflot Airlines Office was almost directly across the hall from my room. She must have dashed straight out of my room and into their office, which had been shut down for the day. Whoever was in charge of the plan to discredit me, the Airline Aeroflot was somehow involved. I assumed the door had been left unlocked in case she needed such a hasty retreat.

Was she a member of the KGB? Possibly. And if so, they had paid Aeroflot for the use of their office. I took little thought of the incident. The KGB is notorious for such entrapments of foreigners. You can be sure that if some attractive, stylish lady makes advances, it is some how masterminded by the KGB.

"You must be very careful when going behind the Iron Curtain," I had been warned. "The Russians are hungry for spies. If the KGB can get you to commit an indiscretion or illegal act, they will film it and use it to blackmail you later."

Life can be very harsh in Communist countries, and lonely too, for a foreigner a long way from home. I thanked God that He was my comforter. I didn't need anything the KGB had to offer.

Chapter 17

Ambassador Robert Strauss

I liked my job meeting important heads of state, religious leaders, and the occasional star. They were the extra bonuses of my ministry. I'd had the good fortune of an introduction to President George Bush.

His smile was relaxed, but his voice carried the note of authority. In laymen's terms, I felt I'd earned my wing commander's pay, but the money hadn't come in yet.

The fax line opened up a relationship between me and the White House which offered us both amenities. My messages to him offered insight into events, situations that arose in my travels. Sometimes I got word back, sometimes I didn't. A lot depended on the gravity of the matter.

The stress of his profession was showing on him, and noticeably so. His black bush of hair was beginning to show a little gray, hardly unusual for a man of his age. Every day I thanked God for my blessing of health, remembering those first years in the ministry, the formative years. I realized how much more comfortable I was now with me, even if I did feel especially tired this trip.

I found out that the White House did not send a message to Ambassador Robert Strauss in Moscow that Chris Panos was arriving in Moscow.

"That's quite a surprise," I replied, when I learned that Senator Phil Gramm, another Texan, had not requested that Strauss help me set up meetings with Mr. Yeltsin.

"The information is not confirmed as yet, but we will have it soon, by the weekend."

Arriving in Moscow on time, I journeyed through customs. I walked outside and arranged for a taxi. It was raining bullets when I arrived at the hotel. I slapped the moisture from my trench-coat and stepped hurriedly into the hallway. A man in a well-pressed business suit bumped into me.

"Oh, excuse me," I said.

"Why are you in this area, and who are you?" he asked.

"You must be security. My name is Chris Panos. Do you know when Mr. Jim Baker is expected?" I opened up my billfold and offered him my identification.

"He's here already." He flashed a surprised look. "Did you just arrive? The suites have been taken up by the press and security. I'm not sure you will get a room."

"I have some inside pull, but thanks," I said as I hurried down the hall. I was hoping that Anna, my friend and an employee of the hotel, was on duty. In the past I had been impressed with her impeccable service and had taken time to report her excellent work to her immediate supervisor. The next visit through, I found that she had been promoted to the position of supervisor. She became a loyal friend. As I cleared the corner, I saw her in her usual place of authority, at the front desk. Anna was blonde, blue-eyed, stood at 5' 3" and weighed 120 pounds. She was a very attractive young lady.

"Anna, do you have my room?" I asked the drone of voices. The place was a madhouse. Three bellhops stood in close proximity waiting for their next duty call.

She looked down at the reservation sheet. "Oh, Mr. Panos, with all the people, they have downgraded you. Let me see if I can find something else." A few phone calls later she had me upgraded to a suite.

"I apologize," she said with a smile. "I wish I could do better, but the hotel is packed." She was her usual self, efficient and apologetic.

"No problem." I thanked her for what she did accomplish. I spoke to the bellhop. "Would you please take the bags up to my room?"

I hurried over to the American attaché, hastily approaching the lady at the desk. "Pardon me, my name is Chris Panos."

She responded, "My name is Betty Champion."

I said, "Could you call the embassy and see if I have any messages?"

"Oh, Sir. There are so many messages. They are reaching the ceiling at the embassy. It would be impossible to track down. Mr. James Baker, Secretary of State, arrived today in Moscow and is staying at the Radisson. The hotel has only been open for two days and it's an absolute mad house." The Radisson was offering a special discount rate. My eyes drifted through the lobby, which was chock full of people jostling and bustling into one another. You could hear the languages of Greek, Russian, American, Italian and Japanese. The lobby was gorgeous. There were Persian carpets in front of the reservation desk. I turned around and saw the contemporary furnishings, the espresso bar, and a beautiful, modern staircase that spiraled upward to the mezzanine. The floors were marble, imported from Greece. It was fabulous.

My eyes came back to the young Betty Champion who was serving as an attaché for the United States government. I nodded in understanding. "But it's very urgent," I stressed.

She said, "What is the nature of your urgency?"

"It is urgent that I meet with Ambassador Robert Strauss. I need his advice desperately."

She laughed. "Oh, is that all?" She pointed over my shoulder. "He's standing right behind you."

I looked across the crowded lobby. He must have overheard the conversation or seen the pointing gestures of our hands. He motioned for me to come over.

"Well, there's another fellow Texan," he said above the crowd, as I thrust my way through. I had been here on another occasion, but by far this was the busiest I had ever seen the hotel. A table was set up close by to serve you, so I grabbed a cup and headed on across.

"You ought to come up north where we could really crown you a superb Texan, you know up north in Dallas?" he said as I walked over to shake his hand. Ambassador Strauss is from Dallas.

"Come sit." He leaned closer so no one else could hear. "I'm about to be interviewed by CBS."

Wolf Blitzer was there with CNN and Tom Mintier. I was introduced to all the key media people. I had met Wolf Blitzer on the London flight to Moscow. There wasn't much time before they were to go on air, but he asked me to sit with them on the couch where they were exchanging small talk.

"That information is obviously of great interest to my negotiating team," Strauss said, "but I find it most surprising in view of the briefings of this morning."

I had no idea what in the world they were discussing. It was an informative first few minutes, even though I seemed to be gleaning only bits and pieces. The media were their usual selves. There was the question-and-answer tennis match, and a few not-so-tactful questions posed as a toss-out for the negotiating team. I listened and laughed to myself. What was a preacher from Texas doing sitting in on this meeting? I caught a few key points, but mostly it was for formality.

Something came out of the meeting for me, though. In the flight from London to Moscow I met Wolf Blitzer, correspondent of CNN, and Rashid K. Barwani from the family Sultanate of Oman.

After the meeting, Robert Strauss asked to be excused and we moved off by ourselves where we could talk.

"I need to visit with Boris Yeltsin," I said hurriedly.

"I will do what I can. We will get some introductions set up for you, as quickly as possible," he came back.

We talked about the affairs of Russia and the U.S.S.R. Soviet block countries. Ambassador Strauss said, "Chris, how much time do you have on your visa?"

I responded, "I have a multi-visa for all the Soviet block countries including Georgia, and I could get my Russian visa extended if need be." I said, "Mr. Ambassador, I would like to meet with Boris Yeltsin," and about that time someone called out to Mr. Strauss.

He gave me a quick apology and patted me on the shoulder. "I have your room number. We will get in touch with you."

He started to turn and I said, "Remember, Mr. Strauss, I have some extra time that I could stay in Moscow in order to meet with Boris Yeltsin."

"We'll get it set up for you, Chris," he said with a big smile. I could see why they trusted him to be Ambassador. He was a man that would get things done. Good news travels fast.

I met a millionaire, the C.E.O. of Aegean Petroleum, Demetries Melissanidis from Athens, Greece. He said, "I overheard you speaking to Mr. Strauss. Come over and have an espresso coffee with me." I was encouraged by his kindness and generosity. He said, "Chris, what about some cookies, Danish roll, and little sandwiches?" and he took one of each and put it on my plate. He said, "Could I order you anything else from the menu?" He was about forty-five, handsome, with black hair meshed with gray trim over his sideburns and black eyes. "Your conversation was very inspired. It seemed to me that when I heard you speaking I received great peace. I would like to visit with you further. Maybe we can go to dinner. Or when are you coming to Greece again? When you do, please remember you're my guest."

I said, "Demetrius, I will remember this invitation." He was very well-mannered and he told me he had to go to be interviewed on Moscow television on how he became a millionaire and why he was willing to invest in Russia at this time. Jokingly he spoke to me, "I have ships that transport oil and I am interested in real estate and especially hotels."

This was a positive opportunity. I wondered what this man's real motive might be. God knew. In His timing it would be revealed. I came to the Radisson to get contacts and introductions form Ambassador Robert Strauss, but God, in His timing, was opening other avenues.

Chapter 18

Is That Your Bag?

Time rushed by like images out of a train window. My hair was turning gray. The hint of age was in my eyes. Yet my desire to go out and win the world for Christ was increasing, not decreasing. I attributed it to spiritual exercise. When a Christian fails to engage in spiritual exercise, to his regret, he will find he had lost standing and power with God.

It was November 1992. We were back in Moscow. Upon arrival, we were required to work with Menshikov again. My feelings were the same. I didn't trust him. I offered him only bits of information, the things I didn't pass on. I knew I must check him out.

Perception had brought changes in me as well as within the structure of the Communist Party that was in the throes of change. Some days I'd say to myself, "Why are you still carrying Bibles, Panos? Aren't the hard times about over?" My ministry and outreach were changing like the world economics. In my heart I knew there could never be a complete turn-around no matter how much the free people of the world prayed for it to happen.

I was thinking back to that first meeting with Yuri Menshikov. Earnestine must have been reading my mind.

"So now what is your assessment?" she said to me that bright, sunny morning. "Are you feeling any better about him? I mean, after all this time working with him, and particularly now at the close of this trip?"

Her question drew a shrug. "My hunch is the same. No matter how much paint he applies to his house, it is still a clapboard house

89

to me. Besides, he isn't the only one I'm concerned about." I was referring to the bald-headed man who had been following me for months. I was beginning to suspect that he was on our side and overseeing me so that I did not come to harm. That is until I would see his menacing eyes following me.

Menshikov was gracious. Offering services well in advance of any request on our part. When God informed me to withdraw, I could withdraw. Irina Yurchenko, our interpreter, had some kind of connection with Menshikov. My contacts said the two had worked together in the past. Whatever their connection, I knew the Russians were not hospitable. They did not inconvenience themselves unless there was something in it for them. During our extended stays, some days we were around in Menshikov's rented vehicle. Some days he would drive up in the vehicle that belonged to the Baptist Church. This day, on our approach for a flight home, he picked us up in his own vehicle.

The sky was dark and ominous like it might dump buckets of moisture any second. He zipped through the parking lot coming to a complete stop a few yards from the entrance.

We were running late.

"Looks like they're short on staff again," he groaned as he crawled from the car.

"I'm still carrying that express invitation from Yeltsin," I said sheepishly. "It's a little dirty, and a little worn, but possibly it would keep us from standing in those long lines?" The words were cautiously dispensed. I felt we were inconveniencing him when I saw him there taking a head count.

"All I want to do is get these bags on the airplane and fly out of here," I repeated.

He looked mildly agitated. I assumed he did not like being put on for favors, unless of course he was the one doing the initiating. "If you have the letter on you, they might make an exception," he said finally.

I patted my breast pocket indicating where I had my visa and the invitation that I had tucked inside for safe-keeping. He disappeared around the corner, leaving us to observe the politics at customs.

For years we had been passing through customs. For years God had been protecting us as we prayed a hedge around us, and angels came to take charge of the airwaves around about us. Those same angels did take charge, but the KGB continued their business of harassment as well.

Just as we approached the check-in area, a mob of people debarked a plane and were met by a ghastly sight: passengers clamoring over one another, watching as their personal belongings were being ripped open, pilfered through, and tossed to the ground. Their stoic faces mirrored the thoughts, but most were too fearful to say anything.

"Is that your bag?" growled the customs agent to the little Jewish lady not twenty feet from us. He pointed to her dark gray piece of luggage as he shot a menacing glare over his shoulder. I didn't usually quake in my boots, but I must admit the darkly sinister eyes, as blue as the sapphire ring on his finger, sent a cold chill down my spine. The whole scene reminded me of an old war movie. It's seen on French television. An American GI stood looking out across the landscape at an imposing army, his eyes full of surprise. For those not schooled in French, a caption below it read very eloquently, "Merci!" Quite a fitting response, I thought, equal to what I was feeling.

Nothing in customs or these agents' lives had changed in years. There was no guilt attached to their actions, at least not anymore. Espionage had brought its own kind of needed excitement. Possibly at first there was guilt, but years of being involved with the evil had given way to a sick kind of enjoyment.

The suitcases, opened and strewn over the entire area, were being scrutinized. Every single bag. Some twice. The decision depended mostly on the nationality of the traveler. Many Jews were on the flight.

The Jewish lady edged forward awkwardly. I wasn't close enough to be of any help, but I prayed silently for the strength of Samson so she could endure. There were troubles ahead.

Her clothing spoke of poverty. It was old and tattered. She was heavyset in appearance. The hair denoted the 1920's. The coat was frayed around the edges. Probably a relic of grave importance once. Rachel Heinzlov was her name. Rachel was very proud to be Jewish. At last she was leaving Russia and going to Israel.

"What do you have to declare, Madam?" barked the customs agent with an unforgiving glare.

She tried to tell him she did not understand. In his impatience he grabbed for her, missed, and caught hold of her jacket. A button popped off and flew through the air like a paper plane in school. It dropped to the floor not five feet away. After years of being made to feel inferior, the lady suddenly found the strength to fight back. A tug-of-war erupted. He won. The last time he reached for her, he tore her blouse and her breast was bare and naked. He found a handkerchief with gold coins wrapped in a knot hidden between her breasts. He took the gold coins and put them in his pocket. The people standing around were too much in shock to say anything or come to her rescue. The faces anguished and turned red, saying it all.

I was shocked and sickened at the show of authority—nothing new for my eyes, except it was now the nineties, not the sixties. Suddenly I remembered the item inside my suitcase. "They must not search our luggage, Lord," I said in a whisper.

"What did you say?" whispered Earnestine.

"The new manuscript is in there."

She looked like she could hardly believe my words. "Why would you bring the manuscript?" she groaned, trying to keep it to a whisper.

Did I have to defend my actions to my own wife? "People risk everything, even their lives, to give me this private information. The secret is to make sure their names are being changed or omitted. God will take care of it. I stared straight ahead and prayed. This time my prayer was deliver this Jewish lady. I knew how cruel the customs agent could be once they were agitated. It was no secret still being used even now and before all of these witnesses.

Growing wary of the situation, the agent screamed out another command and yanked at her with one thought in mind: retrieving her valuables. Obviously he didn't care what he had to do to get them. They scuffled. His hand connected with her cheek. She yanked back in stunned silence. He reached for her again. This time his hand caught the nape of her neck, catching hold of her blouse. Whether he purposely meant to or not, the blouse ripped open, exposing her naked body for the whole world to see. Then the custom agent motioned for him to pass through customs. Rachel was penniless, yet free to return to the Promised Land. She walked away to the departing area to board El Al's Israel's airline for Israel.

Chapter 19

The Romanian Connection

The cruel treatment Rachel received at customs brought my memory back to 1967. The travel brochures stated autumn is the best time of the year to visit Bucharest. It wasn't fall, I hadn't planned my itinerary, and most assuredly I wasn't a tourist. It was mid-January, early on in my Bible smuggling days. Earnestine wasn't with me. The children needed her at home. The weather was typical Black Sea winter: cold and blustery. I boarded the flight from Gdansk, Poland, on the Baltic heading toward Frankfurt to gather my "teaching literature." When I was in the area, I usually stayed with some old friends, the Lofferts, who had been like a second family to me.

"Would you speak in our little congregational church?" Mrs. Loffert asked.

"So how do I turn you down?" I asked. She had such a special way of encouraging me. The offer proved to be a time of refreshing, something I needed since I had been traveling extensively. I always felt honored when asked to share what God was doing in my life. The stop-over evolved into a time of rest and recuperation, a term synonymous with a soldier who has been on the front lines too long, equal to my feelings, considering my last few months of traveling as a "double agent." The church welcomed me heartily, but I was cautious. I spent time in prayer and fasting, and set aside free time for walks. It had been weeks since I had seen Earnestine. I called her.

"The trip's been planned for some time," I said, pausing, thinking about my immediate needs. "I'm just not sure if I'm supposed to be making this trip right now."

"Is something wrong, Chris?" came her reply, her manner questioning.

I've got a backlog on printed Bibles that have not been delivered yet. "They say they are on the way. You know how that can go." As long as I had been in the business for the Lord, sometimes I reacted like the disciples, more specifically Peter. I wanted things to happen in a millisecond from initial prayer request.

"Everything is fine on the home front, Chris." Earnestine was trying her best to reply cheerfully, obviously to convince me that for whatever reason I was still in Germany was okay with her.

We talked a few minutes about unimportant things. It would have been much easier at times, if someone other than myself could make the determinations about my immediate decisions.

"And the children, are they okay?" I asked. Even though I was away from home a lot, Earnestine and the children were in my thoughts every day.

I stood in a phone booth in the lobby of the Dzhierzhinsky Hotel gazing out the window at the snow-covered topography. In the snowy streets in the distance, I caught sight of a young man. He seemed to be observing me. He looked away quickly. A hint of recollection came. I remembered the night before, sometime around dinner, I had observed the same gentleman crossing the street in front of my hotel— nothing big or momentous, but for me something to take note of. His manner denoted a polished dignitary. I had been warned to "never risk being seen in places I had no logical place to be, and to be with someone that I had no logical reason to know."

"Chris, are you still on line?"

I felt like I should know him. "I'm still here. I'm being evaluated from afar."

"Something to be concerned about?" she asked.

"It's nothing. Don't worry!"

Earnestine and I talked only a few minutes more and hung up. We had long since learned to glean information from short catches of conversation. I hung around only briefly. My observer had vanished without a trace.

My next scheduled stop was to be Bucharest, in Romania, often called the "city of gardens." The city itself boasted of the majestic Carpathian Mountains as a backdrop. I took great pleasure in my visits there. The city offered visitors aesthetic vistas, and of course their famous cuisine. It brought visions of a delicacy that always made my mouth water: sarmale (meat and rice wrapped in sauerkraut leaves). Even Bible smugglers get hungry on location.

The country, no bigger than the size of Oregon, had one major asset: variety. I liked that description. It reflected much about the country and its people.

Coming into Romania by air, the landing point is almost certainly to be Bucharest, rightly called the Paris of the Balkans. My flight had progressed as planned. I sat absently thumbing through an old magazine. A model of the spaceship Vostok-1, in which the world's first space flight performed in 1961, flashed up from the page. I mused at the updated technology the Soviet Union had, and yet their total inability for providing information on up-to-date events to their citizens.

"Looking at this," I said, leaning over to talk to the elderly gentleman sitting next to me on the plane. "As a connoisseur of history, I get goose bumps every time I fly into this region."

The little man laughed. "I, too, look forward to seeing the sights and meeting the people again."

I scratched my chin. "I've heard some say this is the area for romance. What do you think?"

"I was born here." He looked blankly out across the wide expanse of land. "It doesn't look romantic to me." He was silent for a moment. "And what is your name?" He turned, adjusting his glasses.

"You haven't heard of me, but that doesn't matter. I'm a businessman from Houston." I paused, wondering if I should offer a further explanation. "My trip, though initially to deliver Bibles, is also for business contacts."

I noted his lifted brows as I remembered my beginnings as a businessman. I'm sure God was not especially pleased with my early business dealings, back before Jesus appeared to me in that hospital room on my death bed and called me to "take His Gospel to the world." But by the grace of God, I was being able to accomplish it, I thought. "What is your name?" I asked. The little man seemed lost in thought, possibly by something I had said.

"Gestalt, Harry Gestalt." He stuck out his hand.

"I like that. You seem to be one of those intensely Francophile relatives." I could see the buildings now, and the rivers in the distance.

"My family comes from there, on my mother's side. There are many similarities between the two capitals. The history books emphasize that the capitals are too similar to be coincidental," said Gestalt.

"I would agree. Bucharest, like Paris, offers many similarities like an Arch of Triumph, leading to Victoriei-Kiseleff, a broad, tree-lined boulevard which resembles the Champs-Elysees."

He stared absently at me, looking like he wanted to ask something. "What do you do for contacts? Surely people do not just appear?"

"Sometimes they do, but when that is not so, I go into East Germany, or any of the German influenced countries. At times Czechoslovakia or Poland.

"Oh, Romania's other leading tourist attraction," he said with an all-knowing smile. "I know about the place. The people of the Soviet Union go there to vacation. By the way, I have an aunt in Moscow."

"I have many friends in Moscow helping me, but there is an overwhelming amount of work to be done there."

"Do you ever regret time spent in this endeavor?" His eyes were big and questioning.

"There are rewards," I said, thinking about his statement. There were rewards, like the peace at the end of a day, or arising to a glorious sunrise to pray and talk to the Lord.

Chapter 20

Under The Hat

"How did you get an aunt in Moscow?" I asked.

He smiled recalling a funny incident. "She ran off and married... against my grandmother's wishes. And you know what? I never liked the woman. When I hear the stories of Moscow, I kind of smile and figure she got her due. Locked in that Siberian wilderness."

His thick accent, coupled with his stories, could send a bolt of laughter through any crowd, and I had seen them all.

"Do you have family in Romania?" I asked, hoping for a long explanation. He was an expert at storytelling, reminding me of an uncle I had as a child.

"Oh, I have a cousin there. I get pictures from her on occasion." His laugh was genuine. "She is not much, how you say, to look at."

"Are all your family members female?" I said with an amused laugh. He nodded. "I've spent time in Romania. I remember the warmer months. It comes alive with fun things to do, not to mention the delicious food."

I pressed back in the seat, remembering those little ice cream wagons that hawked their old- fashioned sugared cones. He must have been reading my mind, for he laughed as if remembering, too.

"Yes," he said with his strange little accent. "The old businessman with a leather-like wrinkled face looked so tired his clothes were ragged and worn. He had a definite way of cleaning the tourist's pockets. What about the creamy delights?"

"Sinful," I said with a laugh.

Romania was the place I went to for new contacts. Flashes of fat little people running around in the 1920's style suits, spending their money, zipped through my mind.

"My cousin sends me pictures, updating what is going on. Russians who have money go there to spend it."

I nodded in agreement just to let him know I was still listening. My mind was wandering the streets, calling out to the vendors.

"What exactly do you do?" he asked, suddenly quite serious.

"I carry God's Word to the far corners of the world. I carry it to Moscow, to the hamlets, and even the beaches in Romania. The harvest is bountiful there!" I settled back in my seat trying to get comfortable, feeling God had something of importance to say to this man.

"How do you make your contacts?" he asked as if being prompted.

"I walk the bright, sunny beaches looking for people to talk to. When I find a mindful soul, I pull off my hat and hold it in my hands. I pull out a Bible, but I keep it well concealed from the authorities, but not the public. Then I just stroll around and point to it. I always draw a crowd. Once I have their attention I begin to talk to them about Jesus."

"What do you say?"

"Jesus has something to say to you through His personal word, something that cannot be intercepted by the KGB."

The little man was glued.

"'Come hear about a man who can change your life,' I say, and the vacationers stop to listen, hanging on my every word. I'm not sure if they are nosey or what. In other areas, even in Russia, this would not be the proper introduction. But the people in this region are quite receptive. Somewhere between the introduction and my first paragraph, and the Bible under that hat, they grab an interpreter, which is always my open invitation to share Christ."

"But what language do you speak?"

"I can speak fairly discernable Russian. I speak it when I can. With this 'under the hat' act, I have stumbled onto the perfect opportunity to reach the Russians, Germans, and Czechoslovakians alike. When the subtleness of the situation hits home, they do not even hate me for it." I laughed. "The interpreter speaks a language that they all can understand."

Gestalt was holding on to every word.

"Harry, there's an innate need inside all of us to reach out to a Holy God." I could see Harry was no exception. "The vacation produces a discontinuity to their otherwise hurried lifestyles. It slows them down, and they listen. It's exciting times, Harry. I continue to use it."

The pilot came on the intercom. "Please keep your belts fastened. We are coming into turbulent weather. We have been detoured to Constanza."

My countenance dropped. I looked out the side window. What was this? I had appointments to keep in Bucharest. I closed my eyes and prayed for the weather to be loosed so God's plan might not be hindered. The weather worsened. A few minutes later I was praying out loud. Even Gestalt bowed his head offering up his own special prayer. I wondered if it was his first in a lifetime, or a renewed interest in it after our conversation?

On approach to Constanza, as the plane began its decent, something started to go haywire. The old bullet of a plane began to shudder like a dog shaking fleas. The wheels bounced, hitting the runway. Then the body of the plane swerved sideways. When it connected, it hit the pavement with a thud and rolled forward on its landing gear. The passengers' faces reflected terror.

"It'll be okay," I said, taking authority.

The plane shuddered once more, like a belch, and then came to an abrupt stop. Those stories you hear about being prayed up? I had been prayed up for years. I even knew which direction I was heading. But right this minute it didn't seem the most fitting time for the invitation. I smiled, releasing a sigh, but not for my audience. It was for the fact that there were too many questionable events to this detour—too many, in fact, to be pure coincidence. I heartily thanked God for our safety and for the opportunities about to be opened to me. It was apparent to me that God had other plans for me than Bucharest.

Chapter 21

Tikanis, Tikanis, Mr. Panos

Although Harry seemed reluctant to shake my hand as we were exiting the plane, he did, and we said a quick goodbye. I said a farewell to our time together and the noise and confusion aboard the plane, forgetting everything but the arctic air that snatched my breath away. I heard the gasp that traveled through the crowd as a literal wall of snow converged on us. I hoped I was going in the right direction. I was doing good just to be able to see a few paces ahead. The passengers were stumbling over each other.

Then it happened. If you have never stood in quiet obedience, feeling the overpowering sense of oneness with God and the universe, I doubt I can give insight into what I was feeling. To better explain, it was like a deep acknowledgment of contentment, like I was at the right place at the right time and something right was about to happen.

We were being half-dragged, half-shoved along with the crowd to customs, and they quickly whisked us on through. I wondered if we were at the right terminal. The agents must have been as cold as we were. Suddenly I heard a voice. A man came running up to me, yelling in Greek.

"Tikanis, Tikanis, Mr. Panos," he said, which meant "how do you do?"

"Are you speaking to me?" I said as I looked back over my shoulder to see who he might be speaking to. I'd had the opportunity of meeting thousands of people in my travels, with many prearranged introductions from the Lord, but I had no recollection of ever having met this gentleman before.

Between chattering teeth, I replied back to him in his native language, "What is your name?"

"Pete. My name is Pete," he said, eagerly sticking out his hand.

I took it. Pete was dressed in a dingy old greatcoat. An inch of snow decorated his shoulders, attesting that he had stood for some time waiting for someone. His smile was genuine. I wasn't sure why he was here, calling out my name in the middle of the storm, but I wasn't about to turn down anything that looked like a friendly gesture.

"How do you know who I am?" I asked as the crowd of people pushed against us. The noise made it almost impossible to hear his response.

"I read it, on your label." He pointed to the bag I had carried with me on the plane. The print was very small.

"I recognized that the name was Greek," he said, smiling proudly.

I laughed, not believing him. How cold he possibly have read anything in that raging storm outside? I reached and began gathering up my bags. Why was he here? The question was short-lived when he leaned over and hefted my biggest bag to the top of his shoulder.

"Do you believe in miracles, Pete?" I asked, smiling, looking his direction, then back to the on-rushing crowd as we proceeded forward.

"I'm a Communist, Mr. Panos," he replied with a set expression, as if his answer alone would suffice. I couldn't help but notice the shoulders. They stiffened against the cold, or could it have been my question?

"Even Communists believe that sometimes events are out of their control," I said gruffly.

He looked up with a satisfied expression. "Now out of control? That I understand," he replied with authority.

Pete was a little man of about five foot two inches, jolly and good-natured. He was quite a talker and had hit on a subject we could both agree on, and we talked briefly as we made our way through the pressing crowd.

"Pete," I said later, when we had moved on through the terminal area. "Do you know where I might find other Greeks to get in touch with around here?"

He repositioned my bag on his shoulder and smiled. "I can probably help you with that."

Chapter 22

Big Fat Zero

By now Pete and I were jogging to help preserve what little warmth there might have been clinging to our bodies. I think my new acquaintance was a little more prepared for the frigid air than me.

"Are you booked into a hotel yet?" he yelled over the drone of fellow passengers following along behind.

"No. This was not my scheduled stop. I was flying into Bucharest before the storm." I waved at the bright yellow taxi, which screeched to a halt alongside us. For a brief moment I felt like we were being watched. I scanned the immediate area and beyond, taking in every moving and non-moving entity within twenty years, and secretly examined my newfound friend in the process. My premonitions were usually on target. Pete had to be a KGB agent. Why else had he been thrust into my path?

"Your appearing when you did was a blessing," I said, as we climbed into the taxi. "I had no one waiting for me this stop." I watched out of the corner of my eye for a response. Receiving none, I went on. "I don't know about you, but I could use a hot bath and a good dinner."

Pete leaned over informing the driver where to take us. "Since you are Greek, Mr. Panos, what do you think of the Greek Orthodox Church?"

The question was loaded from the start, and from his tone of voice, I assumed he had a special vendetta against the church or a person connected to it.

"I'm a member. And you?" It wasn't a valid question, I knew it.

"I'm a Communist," he replied with guarded but staunch conviction, as if playing before an audience. He sat silent for a few moments. When he did speak, he had regained his composure.

Clearing my throat, I searched for the right and correct entry. "We all believe in something, Pete, especially when things begin to unravel around us."

He mumbled, "Something is pursuing you."

I said, "Or when a loved one dies. Where do you turn then?"

He looked up, startled, as if I was reading his thoughts.

"Are you running from someone?" I asked. He didn't answer. "Who knows what we might reach out for when facing the fear of capture or imminent death?" My voice had dropped to a whisper. "I've been there, Pete." I was breaking the rules, as far as Communists are concerned. They liked being in control and asking the questions. "Years ago, Pete, in the middle of the night, my mother was gravely sick from complications of my birth. They wheeled her down a long corridor at John Sealy Hospital in Galveston, Texas."

I thought back on the story that had been told me so many times. "It was a hot day, the 25th of August, a few years after the stock market crash of 1929. The doctor minced no words to my father.

"'I don't think I can save both your wife and your child. Tell me what to do,' said the doctor.

"Painfully my father thought about it. 'Save my wife,' he said finally.

"'Perhaps we can try again,' said the doctor."

As I began to relate my story to Pete, my life played before me like in the movies. Suddenly I saw my childhood and the growing-up years. Some of it had been painful. I saw myself as a father, and as a businessman, remembering well the man in the boot business... my first business beginnings. I recalled the time spent in the air conditioning business. And equally as grievous, I saw the drunkard, the man who would rather have been out drinking than at home with his beautiful wife. I wanted to shut off the ugly pictures.

By this time, I wasn't sure what was fact or fiction, what was being spoken out loud or remembered with mental pictures. I was grateful God had taken me out of the debauchery, but in my mind's eye I saw it all as if it was yesterday. I don't believe it is ever easy to see the bad, much less share it with some perfect stranger, but sometimes that segment of life can be needful to a searching heart. It can relate what God can do if given the opportunity. I must have been some raw nerves. The man who sat beside me in that taxi listened intently, absorbing my accounts with a contrite expression.

"I remember standing at the cash register in my boot shop," I went on. "On many occasions some poor indigent person would wander into the shop and ask me for help. I didn't want them in my establishment. I didn't care who they were. I didn't care about anyone. In my self-appointed state of righteousness, I felt they needed to look for their money or pity elsewhere. I certainly wasn't going to have pity on any wino asking for a handout, and most assuredly I didn't want them asking for it from me! Money was my god."

Pete studied me. He was as quiet as death.

"Members of the wife's prayer group came entreating me to find some elusive God they kept talking about. The Greek Orthodox Priest came with lottery tickets, which I bought. It was a good deed and made me feel better momentarily. At least it made me look better to the priest. It didn't help. It all seemed wrong somehow." I looked over at Pete, wondering why I had felt led to offer him these confidences. "But you know what, Pete?" I swallowed hard. "At that point, my life amounted to a big fat zero!"

His eyes were wide and expressive, following mine.

"Hell is just a commute away from the residential and industrial side of our character... about one kilometer from the ragged edge," I said with finality.

Pete released a deep sigh.

"A vision appeared to me, Pete. Suddenly I saw a big black puff of smoke, and a voice thundered from that cloud of black sinful nothingness, saying, 'Chris Panos, I saved you from death in that car accident when you were at death's door, and now you are going to become a millionaire. The desires of your heart are going to be yours, and all you have to do to attain it is to bow down to me.'

"No sooner had the voice finished speaking than a light came from out of nowhere, piercing through the darkness of the cloud, and a stronger, sweeter, kinder voice projected from the brightness. At first I couldn't understand then it came clear. 'Chris Panos, you will live. I have saved you for my own. You have a story to tell for me.'

"That voice commanded attention and expressed itself in Greek, saying, 'Soteria' (meaning saved, fully and completely, in every area of your life, spirit, soul, and body)."

When I finished, Pete's eyes bore an emotion I had not seen in them before.

"God gave me a new life, Pete. He can do that for you, too."

After a moment of silence Pete said something under his breath. He saw I did not hear him. "I'm a practical man, Mr. Panos. I do not need this God you speak about... besides, how could a..." He stopped cold.

I assumed he was about to share his involvement with the KGB. Assumed he was about to say how could a Communist KGB agent find a holy God?

He cleared his throat. "I'm a Communist."

"God in His sovereignty visited me that night, Pete. If He has not shown Himself to you, wait. He will... He can forgive, even a Communist."

Chapter 23

Sima

Over the years God kept extending my area of ministry. He opened a special television ministry in Houston, Texas, called "The Chris Panos Show." Our program came on television every day. Many blessings were born out, also many contacts and new friends in the Lord. It was how we met Sima, who later Earnestine and I befriended.

Sima was a former Russian citizen, then living in Houston with doubts about her quick release from captivity. In her heart she felt the KGB was still lurking around every corner trying to catch her in a fault. Shevchenko, the Ukrainian writer, said, "It is terrible to fall in prison and chains, but it's much worse to sleep in liberty." He was a Russian and must have known both.

Americans live on Apple Pie Lane, eat cherry pudding, and seldom if ever have any real threat to their life. We have no concept of prison or chains, whether it is physical or mental.

God was gracious with our ministry. With the television program in the talk show format, anyone with a need was encouraged to call in. Every day we were flooded with calls.

"Hello. Welcome to the Chris Panos Show," we'd say as we opened our lines. "If you need something, please call," said Earnestine with her more-than-welcoming invitation every morning and particularly that morning.

There was an immediate call. When Earnestine picked up the phone, she heard heavy breathing, but the party refused to say anything. It wasn't the first. We'd been receiving these calls for a week now. Either the person couldn't speak English or was afraid to speak. The receiver went dead. A second later the phone rang again.

"Good morning, may I help you?" said Earnestine in her soft, cheerful voice again. At first she wondered if the caller had hung up, since the line was silent. Finally she heard a faint sound, almost like a whisper.

"Come to me. I am a dangerous woman," said a woman's voice in very broken English. "Come to me!"

Earnestine began to question the caller. "Do you need prayer?" She looked across the aisle at me and the TV cameraman watching from the sidelines.

"No understand," said the voice on the other end of the line.

"Are you sick?" Earnestine asked, phrasing each question carefully. What should she ask next?

"No!" came the woman's reply.

"What is your name?" Earnestine motioned to one of the stage hands to catch the other lines. He quickly picked up the receiver. "Are you a Christian?" asked Earnestine.

"No," said the voice with much finality.

"What is your name?" asked Earnestine again.

"My name is Sima," said the woman barely audible. Her next words came with more volume. "My name is Sima. I am from Russia."

"Do you go to church, Sima?" Earnestine asked, feeling she might be making some progress. What did this woman need?

"I go to synagogue," was her reply. "Come to me. I am dangerous woman."

Earnestine jotted down the woman's address. There was something desperate about the person on the other end of the line. Who was she, and what did she really want?

Earnestine took the address, and after the program she struck out to find the elusive voice who out of total desperation had called into a TV talk show.

Earnestine's eyes scanned the run-down tenements as her car rumbled to a stop. There was little to be said for the neighborhood: broken windows, houses without curtains, an eyesore by any standards. Filth and litter decorated the walkway up to the apartment.

Garbage littered the stairwell. She had to kick trash to the side before she could climb the rickety old stairs. The only window in the stairwell was so dirty it blocked any direct light that might have made its way through making it extremely dark. The one little light bulb that hung in the center of the ceiling was blackened on one side from an electrical malfunction. She finally made it to the door where she had been directed.

She knocked three times and waited. What manner of woman might answer the door? She thought of all the visits to needy people she had made before. She was confident that God had directed her to this person in particular, but she was filled with apprehension.

"Hello," said a small, dark-haired woman, half hiding behind the half opened door. She looked to be about fifty. A young man stood protectively behind. Their expressions were strained.

"Are you Sima?" Earnestine asked kindly, waiting to be given an invitation to come inside.

"Yes. This is my son, Leon. She stepped back. Leon at last stuck out a hand. When Earnestine began to speak, Leon was relieved and invited her in.

"Would you like to be seated?" he asked.

"Yes, I would like that." Earnestine held her Bible tightly in her hand until she sat down, then she lay it on the stool in front of her chair, where it remained like a promise. It wasn't long until Sima loosened up and began to talk.

Chapter 24

People Follow Me and Watch Me

"I was schoolteacher," said Sima. "I became target of espionage." She motioned like someone spying. "I notice it one day when I walk to school. Weeks later I find they follow me every where." She recoiled as if someone were after her even now. "I live in fear."

"But you are in America now."

"No, never mind. They are still there."

"How long have you been here, Sima?"

Sima paid little notice of Earnestine's question. "When the door open, Leon and I leave Russia. We go to Rome for six months where we were taught some English."

Leon broke in. "They trained us to come to America."

"Who trained you? How did you get money to come to America?" Earnestine asked, trying to follow along.

"Funding came from Jewish American Fund. We come to Houston," said Sima as she looked around her tiny apartment. "They furnished us in this place and give income to live on...'till we are able to make it on own."

"But this is a safe place. This is America," Earnestine said again.

"Mother cannot be so sure. I go to school every day, but she is here alone. She sees things."

The apartment was meagerly furnished. Nothing is ever disposed of in a Jewish family. In the far right corner on an old coat tree hung both of their coats, tattered but still useful. The apartment was clean, and they had a telephone.

"Sima, why did you call me? I am unsure what it is you want

from me?" Earnestine said kindly.

Frightened and secretive, she said, "I am being spied upon. Everywhere I go, people follow me and watch me."

It seemed Earnestine could not get through the block, even though she explained once again that she was now in America and could let down that rigid guard. They visited as best they could with Sima's broken English. Sometimes Earnestine had to wait while Sima looked up a word in her dictionary.

"It was terrible. Father exiled until he died. I did not see him again. Everyone knows they are out there. We live in fear," Sima said almost in a whisper.

"Sima, Jesus Christ came to give you freedom, from the past, from your sins, from your fears."

"No understand. No understand," was her response.

Earnestine listened attentively, and before she knew it three hours had passed. It was time to go, but she wanted to leave them with peace of mind.

"Would you allow me pray to the God of Abraham to care for you and Leon?" Earnestine asked sincerely.

Sima's eyes lit up. She remembered that somewhere in her childhood she had heard about the God of Abraham. She nodded.

"Holy God, come to this very place. Slip in beside Sima and Leon and give them your calm assurance. Let them know they have a friend in you." The prayer was short, and when Earnestine had finished, Sima's face was radiant. She had found herself a friend in Earnestine, the lady whose face came across her television set. For some unknown reason, Sima had confidence that she could trust this lady—something very hard for her to accept after so many years of secrecy. This was the first time she had ever met Earnestine face-to-face.

A few days late, Sima called the television station again asking for Earnestine. She asked her to come and visit again. When Earnestine pulled up in front of the apartment, Sima was waiting. The door swung open, and Sima ran out and down the stairs, yelling. "My friend, my friend Earnestine, my very good friend!" She looked happy. She invited Earnestine up. They talked for a long time. Suddenly her mood changed. "They are still spying on me."

Earnestine felt great compassion for Sima and Leon. They had no one. I heard the stories secondhand, but we would go to God and petition Him for the two of them.

One night some time later, Earnestine and I had been invited to a friend's house for dinner. We got on our dual phones and dialed Sima's number and asked if she'd like to come to dinner with us.

"Yes," she replied positively.

For a minute I didn't know if she was saying yes, she wanted to come and go, or if she had not understood and was asking me to go on.

"Does that mean you will come and go?" we asked again, now that we were both in on the conversation.

"Yes, Leon and I would like that," replied Sima.

Chapter 25

Sima was Shocked

Leon was excited about going. Earnestine explained that they would have spent the evening home alone otherwise. We made it to our friends. When it came time to eat dinner, Sima took out her big purse. We watched in awe as she pulled out a brown lunch bag and proceeded to open it. Our mouths dropped as she pulled out her and Leon's dinner.

"Oh no, Sima," said Earnestine. "When you are invited to dinner here in America, you do not have to bring your own food." Earnestine's words were gently dispensed for fear of hurting her feelings.

.Sima looked shocked. "No...Sima and Leon have prepared their own dinner." The words were defensive.

The American family looked on in horror. "Is this how it is done in Russia?" they asked.

Sima thought on the question. "In Russia, there is not enough food to go around. We are very selfish."

Earnestine glanced at the other dinner guests. Sima's words brought a new awareness to all of us.

"We set our allotment out and count it cautiously or else we will all starve. I cannot eat your food," she said with great finality as she folded her hands.

Minutes later, when our group was stuffing their faces, with a little coaxing they began to partake, cautiously at first, then eagerly.

When Sima and Leon had eaten their fill, they smiled approvingly. "Never have we eaten such food," they said. They began to loosen up and talk. "I wanted to come to American to learn, then I hoped to go back to Israel to live," Leon said thoughtfully, as if he had researched it quite thoroughly in his mind.

The night was spent in conversation getting to know each other, and over the next few weeks the friendship grew. Earnestine and I continued to ask them to accompany us on many outings. We learned about their love for ice cream and asked them to come to a special ice cream parlor. At the parlor one evening, I was visiting with a black man who worked at the place. We laughed richly, teasing with each other.

"In Russia, we were told whites hated blacks and the like," Sima said, reflecting on the situation. "They also told us blacks never have jobs."

"There's unemployment among all classes of people here in America. The blacks have not had the opportunities like the whites, but it is getting better now," I said, trying to answer her question directly.

Suddenly, for reasons beyond our knowledge, Leon and Sima began to speak Russian. There was an urgency about their conversation.

"Is there something wrong?" I asked, looking directly at Leon.

"We are being watched. The table is bugged."

"Here in America, you are safe. The God of Abraham is watching over you," I replied confidently. They looked puzzled. I added, "He is watching over all of the Jewish people."

"If this is true, when will he avenge the blood of his people?" she replied arrogantly.

There was much lost in the translation. It was impossible for the two of them to fully trust or understand what was being said to them. They still referred to their dictionary, when doubtful of the translation.

One day, after weeks of befriending them, Sima called for Earnestine. When she got to the apartment, Sima was hysterical. Servicemen had arrived to repair her air-conditioner which had been leaking water for over a week. They arrived just before Earnestine did. When they left, Sima turned to her friend. "You, see, this has been leaking for a week. They would not come till they knew you were coming to check on them."

"How would they have known that, Sima?"

"My telephone is bugged. When they hear you were coming, they came to fix it."

Earnestine kept trying to prove to Sima that she was now in America, but in her distraught state, there was nothing she could say to convince her differently. The terror she felt was coming back, and she directed it at us in the form of questions. Most of what she was feeling, the fearfulness, was related to the past, or so Earnestine thought, but the more involved she became with Sima, the more she wondered could there be some truth to her accusations.

Earnestine took Sima to meet Linda, one of her friends who lived near Sima. When Linda noticed Leon's badly worn shoes, she gathered him and Sima and took them to a shoe store close by that was having a sale.

"How much?" Sima asked as she lifted the shoes up to the sales lady.

"If you buy one pair, you get another pair for $1.00."

Sima heard what the man had said, but from her expression she was not convinced they meant it. Linda bought Leon the two pairs of shoes, and Sima became very afraid, fearing Linda might be working for the KGB.

"Why would you want to buy Leon two pairs of shoes?" asked Sima, trying to understand these American ways.

"Because he needs them for school, and they are on sale. I don't want anything in return. This is what we are taught in America," said Linda, but she could see from Sima's expression she could not fathom why anyone would give a gift and expect nothing in return.

Chapter 26

Sima Disappears

Everywhere that Earnestine and Linda went, they took Sima and Leon too, if he was off from school. Sima always took her own food just in case no one would share with her. They were rising in the car one day, and Leon began telling funny stories about the Jews. He had a great sense of humor. And coming from a Jew the story had a more humorous twist.

"One day I was in the community butcher shop," said Leon, straight-faced. "The owner was not Jewish, but he catered to us anyway. Some of my friends came in the door as I was browsing for meat. Stuart, my friend, walked up to the counter and pointed a finger at a new item in the case. It looked very appetizing. 'May I taste this before I buy it?' he asked with newfound authority.

"'Hey Stu, ain't you Jewish?' yelled one of his friends, who wasn't Jewish, from the back of the store. 'I happen to know that's not kosher.'

"'Yeah? Well who asked ya?' he said as he took it from the butcher and ate it." Leon found the story greatly amusing.

The more we got to know Sima, the more Earnestine wasn't sure what Sima needed. When they were together, she seemed to relax and enjoy herself. Yet when Earnestine had to leave, she would withdraw into her shell again. After much thought on this, Earnestine made an appointment with a Rabbi hoping to take Sima to him. She asked if he could have someone to interpret Russian for the meeting that they arranged. He was so interested in helping. His leather-like wrinkles seemed to vanish when he smiled. He was distinguished, head and shoulders taller than most Rabbis. He wanted to help Sima and Leon.

"Would you have someone preferably Russian that might be able to befriend Sima?" Earnestine asked soon into their conversation.

Looking strangely perplexed, he said, "Well, Earnestine, the apartment complex that she lives in has several Russian-Jewish families." He glanced from Sima back to Earnestine. "The problem is, they do not trust their own kind."

"Why? If I were in Russia, I would reach out to my fellow countrymen," Earnestine said with mixed emotion.

"You, my dear lady, have never lived in a country where your neighbor is paid to spy on you, is offered political position for such a fine deed."

They talked for the space of an hour. Sima took it all in, her dictionary occasionally for statements she was not sure of, even though the Rabbi had provided an interpreter. After all, how could she trust this Rabbi? He was of Russian origin. But Sima seemed happier when they left.

Sometimes Earnestine would call Sima on the phone, and she would hardly say a word. What she needed was a friend that could devote blocks of time to her and befriend her and take her places. Earnestine has many responsibilities: children, a husband and a ministry.

One night, a few months after she had gotten to know Earnestine, we had settled in for the evening. When the phone rang, it startled us. People did not usually call so late unless there was trouble. It was Sima, and her first emotion was fear. "Hello, Panos residence," she said with exaggerated composure. "Please come to me. I am leaving in morning."

"Sima, are you okay?" Earnestine asked quickly.

Sima had little to say. Earnestine asked her several other questions that she ignored completely. Not a full two minutes later, they hung up. Earnestine paced the floor and we did consider getting dressed and going over, but to be perfectly truthful, it was not the kind of neighborhood you went into in the middle of the night. The crime rate was rampant. There were constant random murders, rapes. Houston has changed. There are topless clubs in every elite area. One of the clubs is selling more booze than the Astrodome. We are seeing some drive-up killings. They stop at a red light and suddenly will open their window and shoot to kill. Even on the freeways they shoot at passing cars.

"Let's pray for Sima," I said. "I could go with you over there, but you know how funny she is about me being with you." We prayed passionately for Sima that night. And Earnestine sought God for Sima in the middle of the night. Since she had called Sima before, late in the night, and never got an answer, she wasn't really worried because she knew Sima would never accept a call so late.

"If I send a policeman to her door in the middle of the night, Sima would be convinced it was the KGB." We decided to leave it in God's hands.

As soon as we awakened the next day, Earnestine grabbed for the phone and dialed Sima's number. The phone rang and rang. Over the space of an hour she continued to ring Sima's number to no avail. She could not be sure if Sima was there or not. I had a business appointment that I could cancel, but we prayed for Sima again before I left. Earnestine got dressed and went directly to Sima's apartment. She knocked many times but no one answered. She inquired at a neighbor's, but no one had any knowledge about Sima. Sima had told no one about her plans to leave.

We never heard from Sima since that night. Her name has been lifted in my prayer many times over in the span of the years that has followed since that first and last meeting.

Left behind are the fond memories of their laughter, and our memories of getting acquainted, and of course the fun times. There was and still is a vacuum of emptiness. We miss Sima and Leon and still pray for them. And more importantly, may the Holy God of Abraham come to the place you are at, and give you calm assurance, and let you know that He is your "Friend," a friend that will never go away, not even when fear makes you want to run away.

Chapter 27

Going To Riga, Latvia

In Moscow alone it is said that almost 40,000 of its top echelon of society have received special treatment by the Communist Party. In America we would call that widespread corruption. This special treatment includes special hospitals, special services, special instructors, even special food. It's a flagrant misuse of power to benefit the Kremlin elite.

This was my main thought when Earnestine spoke to me from her desk that early morning in April of 1990. We had been praying for the right opening to formally pave our way into the Soviet Union, not under the threshold invitation, as in the past.

"What do you think, Chris?" Earnestine was sitting at her desk trying to catch up on mail. "We've been waiting patiently to hear a positive word back. What could possibly take this long for any Russian document to come into place?"

I looked up from my work. "You are asking me a question such as that concerning Russian behavior?" I shook my head. "I have been waiting on the Lord to open doors much too long to start worrying about it now. If God opens the doors, we will proceed with the crusades."

In my spirit I honestly felt the timing was right, but the doors had not yet opened. The phone rang and Earnestine answered it with her normal "hello, may I help you?" voice. "Yes, he is here," she said, smiling. "Just one moment." She waved for me to grab the other line. I heard the booming voice even before I got it to my ear.

"Pack your bags, Chris Panos. We need you to come to Latvia."

Who could have mistaken that laugh, so characteristic of Vassilly? "Only this time, Chris Panos, you will be receiving a handwritten letter at the express invitation of the government."

I jumped to my feet. "Thank you, Jesus! That's what we've been waiting for."

We laughed together and made tentative plans for the crusades. Earnestine sat by smiling, knowing how elated I was over whatever it was I was hearing. "I'll be back in touch as soon as I get all the plans solidified," I said and hung up the phone.

Earnestine was beaming. "I suppose we need to pack your bags?"

"Actually we need to pack our bags." I laughed and hugged Earnestine. "The date's been set if we can put it together from this end. Thank God, Earnestine. Can you believe it? The country that was totally controlled by the Communists, the country where I smuggled Bibles into by sliding in on someone else's coattail, is now extending an open invitation for me to come and bring Bibles and preach the Gospel!"

A few days later when the phone rang I was busy posting at the computer. It rang the third time before I could grab it.

"Mr. Panos, your multiple visa has just been granted."

I was shocked. I had almost given up on it, but the moment he started to speak, I chorused the words of joy along with him. "Yes. Oh yes! Thank you."

"God has perfect timing, don't you think?" echoed Earnestine, who had been standing close by at the file cabinet. We laughed together and gave the Lord credit. This wasn't anything new—getting prayers answered—but even after all these years it was a bountiful blessing when the miracles unfolded for our own benefit.

It's the answer we've been praying for," I said.

We both knew what a multiple visa meant. It meant we would have the freedom to go into any Communist country, even Cuba, where we had been laying plans for a face-to-face meeting with Castro himself.

"You'll have the opportunity to visit Albania, the area walled off from us in the past," she mused, thinking of the implication.

"And Burma, and Vietnam, and all of them," I said, laughing. We had been praying for this for some time.

"How many days?" Earnestine asked. She always had the worst duty, which entailed packing all of our personal things.

"Seven days, maybe ten. There are many loose ends to tie up." The days moved by swiftly.

"The sports stadium has been confirmed," Earnestine said, smiling as I walked into the office that morning.

"Has Vassilly called?" I dropped a bundle of mail on her desk.

"Twice." She picked it up and started going through it. "You have a meeting at the bank at 9:30 today. Something about getting things lined up for easy transfer. Vassilly wants to talk with you." She smiled. "He said he would call back."

The following Sunday, before we finished packing, we knelt down together and prayed for a bountiful harvest of souls. Right there in the middle of our suitcases, strewn across the entire bedroom floor, God brought His assurance once again to our spirits.

The phone began to ring. I knew the phone was somewhere in the room, but in our gusto to pack our things, we had lost it. "Yes, just one moment, please," said Earnestine, when she finally found it. She waved it in the air, motioning for me. "Vassilly," she said.

"Vassilly! Yes. We're in the middle of... packing. Yes, Earnestine is coming. We'll be on our way soon. I'm so glad you called." Earnestine pulled up a chair for me. "I've been thinking. We need to set up meetings to train the nationals. It's something God impressed on me after our crusades in India. Training the people themselves is the only way to assure God's work will go on once the meetings are over."

"It's already done. I just called to tell you we'll meet you at the airport. Hope to see you early." He hung up.

I had never met Vassilly face to face, so I was elated at the prospect. The sports stadium was booked. We were informed that there would be millions of possible viewers throughout the USSR. Two crusades were scheduled for Latvia, one in Siberia, and a possible one in the Ukraine.

Chapter 28

Vassilly, A Heart of Gold

We finally arrived in Latvia. In the cab ride over from the airport, Earnestine and I reflected on past accounts of sneaking through customs with Bibles.

"In times past it took a sovereign act of God, and those first attempts were an awesome burden," I said, smiling, remembering the "good old days."

"I can't believe it. I began as a traveling preacher thumbing my way around the world on a dime. Call it blind faith, and it was on my part, but God never let me down."

"God has let you down, Chris."

"Oh, there were times when I was upset over the lack of expediency, but I learned He was the one in control, and if I had a complaint, I was required to take that up with Him. In those days I was concerned more over my flock. Especially when the secret police hounded my every move." I looked out the window at the geography flying by. "I'd grow weary sometimes and say, 'I quit,' then I realized that there would be no prodigal son parable for a minister who left his flock. He would not be welcomed back. The damages would be permanent, and the locker room closed to this star forever."

"And that's why you are still here."

"One night, about midnight, when I was lamenting about the turn of events and in despair, I cried out, 'Lord!' You know how deeply involved the KGB is into the Baptist Church? If I stay, I am going to have to take an even more fearful stand, questioning the very people who hold my hand."

"But you didn't?"

"Only in a subtle way. God impressed me to follow his bidding. He told me He would take care of the rest."

Over the next few days in Latvia, I received introductions from many fine ministers and lay persons who were attending the crusades. I was also graciously introduced to Antoly Sokalov, a giant in the area of Christianity. But when I was finally introduced to Vassilly, I shook his hand with pride.

Vassilly was a big man, standing six-foot-two, weighing more than a mountain, with a heart about as big. He reminded me of a big old teddy bear.

"Brother Panos," he said. " I want to start a church in Riga. I want you to be the pastor after this crusade."

I laughed, seeing as how he dove for the heart. "Well, Vassilly, that's my ministry, starting churches," I said with equal enthusiasm.

Later that evening at the meeting I was introduced to many different pastors. One came from Surmati located on the Volga River at the beginning of Siberia. Older citizens remember it as Kuybyshev. Another pastor came from Cherkossy in the Ukraine. We had crusades planned for both areas. Over the following days I used every free minute getting acquainted with these godly men and learning all I could about their churches.

"I am humbly impressed," I said to all the pastors when we were together. "There's a beautiful rapport about this group. I see great love begin expressed here among you."

"It's an opportune time for all of us. A time for us to get to know one another," offered one of pastors from Siberia.

The next day all the pastors and doctors of the city were there, along with the medical people. "I'll tell you, Mr. Panos," said Vassilly, "it doesn't seem like the medical profession is fighting us on this— they don't believe that God can heal anyway."

"That makes it an even greater opportunity for me. God has given me a special message for doctors. In all of my travels and introductions, I've met many of the finest doctors in the world. They tell me... 'I can cut out a good organ, and put it back into another body, but after the initial work of the surgery openly God or mother nature can do anything with it from there.'"

"God has brought you here for these meetings," said Vassilly humbly. "It is a much needed message."

I thought on his statement—"God has brought you here." I was asking myself, *Has God brought me here to share the Gospel to mend broken hearts, or am I here to expose the KGB infiltration of the church?* I thought about Menshikov and wondered how many of the seeds I'd so carefully planted he had discovered and destroyed.

What a closeness I found among the brethren. I had never felt it among any other Russian counterpart before. God was opening hearts. I think He was beginning with my own.

Over the following days I brought many timely messages to the city. His spirit descended like a whirlwind, performing miracles and healings. Even though God sends me, sometimes I am as awed as the people to whom the miracles are given. I know it has nothing to do with me or my might or my power, just a Holy God reaching down and anointing His servant to preach His message, so individual hurting hearts might catch hold of His truth and find His healing for their lives.

I preached to packed crowds every night. The highways were full. Days later the messages were then replayed all over the Baltic States on radio and television, twice in the day time, twice at night, then they were rolled over to the USSR where some possible 120,000,000 more viewers might have seen it. Being viewed all over the former USSR was truly an act of God.

Chapter 29

A Snake For Dinner?

After the meeting, Vassilly walked over to Earnestine and myself and smiled. "I've been waiting for the opportunity to talk to you." He looked between us. "I would like for you to be our guests. My wife and I would like for you to come and have dinner with us tonight."

We were delighted. "We would like that very much," we said almost in unison.

"Please come early," he said warmly. "Here's the address. We'll be expecting you around 7:00 p.m."

His home was graciously opened for us that night. Everyone was there: pastors and ministers, friends, and people from all areas of the medical profession. They were very gracious hosts. Once we were seated at Vassilly's table, I looked over at a plate in the center of the elegantly spread table. Obviously the main dish was something of importance, since it held the place of honor. Upon closer inspection I saw it was some kind of a delicacy, specially prepared. They knew I loved fish. Whatever the entree was, it happened to be long and stringy.

Vassilly gave the prayer and began the tradition of passing the dishes. He sent it past Earnestine first. "Would you like to try our specialty dish of the night?" he said with a smile, his eyes glinting mischievously.

Earnestine looked slightly comical, her big round eyes studying the plate that had been slid in under her nose. Never having been daring with her cuisine, she smiled. "I believe I will pass." She said it every so pleasantly, but she did take a little of everything else they offered.

"Yes, I will try some," I said, as it came past. I smiled, accepting it with great anticipation. A few seconds later, after the courses of food had been passed, prayers said, and formalities dispensed, I bit into the "special dish." It tasted strange and looked somewhat like an amputated squid tendril. Upon closer examination I found a perfectly round bone running down the center of it. I wondered what I was eating. I smiled to my hosts, trying to look nonchalant and I inconspicuously searched for the head. After a few tries there is was... and right below it a little circular mouth.

"Oh my," I said, audibly, but under my breath. "This has to be snake."

I looked around to see who might have heard the close of the service and gave his warm salutations. "We have a great blessing for those of you who have come this last night of the crusade. Chris Panos will be at the back of the church handing out Bibles. Say a special hello and get one of your way out."

Oh, what an offer. People running smack up against one another, like sardines neatly tucked in a can. I laid stacks of Bibles of a table and retrieved them from boxes on the floor. A few minutes after I'd caught up with dispensing the merchandise, I managed to slip out to my car for my camera. Upon my return, I stood up as tall as my body could reach. My right arm was outstretched, and I was snapping pictures.

What a sight! People so excited about getting a small New Testament that they had no idea who was even giving them out, nor did they care. Over the years I came to judge God's presence in a meeting by their response to me. If they said glowing words over me afterwards, I worried. If they wept in deep contrition, I knew God had done the speaking.

These people were so hungry for the Word, I rejoiced. Literally hundreds and thousands, possibly more, had heard the Gospel and surrendered their life during this crusade.

I ministered to the crowd. It was heart-rending, but later when I was listening to it being televised over television, I sat alone in my hotel room. I was forced to come face to face with my own message. What a piercing to the core, even to my own heart. I was touched just as the other listeners.

I was reminded of an incident back in Vienna when I had gone through customs. As a brand new Bible Smuggler, God was trying to teach me about fasting and praying. In the hotel room that evening, the Lord impressed me to get on the elevator and go downstairs. With no idea where I was going, I marched down the hallway. A word kept coming to me, but I wasn't sure if it was a word or a name. I kept repeating it over and over under my breath. I approached the front desk, and all I can tell you is it just kind of came out: "Ull."

The desk clerk looked up in surprise. "Is that his first name?" he asked. I shrugged, as if I didn't quite understand. He pulled out the telephone book and began looking through it. "Would it be Rev. Ull?" he asked. I shrugged again. "There is a Rev. Ull of the British and Foreign Bible Society."

I smiled, nodding an affirmative. I grabbed for a pen and jotted down the number. I was sure it was more than a hunch. I prayed it was a direct word from the Lord. I dialed the number. I still had no idea what to expect. A man answered.

"Hello, I'm Chris Panos, a minister from America. God told me to call you."

He paused a second. "Are you looking for Bibles?" he asked, as if he had been sitting waiting for my call.

"How did you know?" I asked, with surprise.

"Last night I had a dream that someone was going to come to me wanting Bibles."

"Well, Rev. Ull, I need Bibles, lots of them."

"Come see me tomorrow. I have plenty."

Chapter 30

Angel of Satan

We arrived at the hotel, took a quick shower, and hurried down to the meeting which was already in progress. They were singing when we walked in. All day I had been deliberating over what message to bring. I had many stirrings on various subjects, but it was now 8:30 p.m. and I had no idea what I was going to preach on. God would truly have to deliver his message for the hour.

As I made introductions, I looked out across the sea of questioning faces. Earnestine's was on the second row shining back at me. Suddenly a voice seemed to speak to me, telling me the words to say.

"Have you ever wondered what it would have been like had the Judges lead a consecrated life?" My voice was eager and quick as I stepped across the podium. You could have heard a pin drop. "We might not have just chapters 13, 14, 15, 16 in the Books of Judges. There may have been 100 or more books."

The crowd looked at me with great puzzlement. Words began to flow like the ocean, magnifying the Lord Jesus, coming down and touching, cold angry hearts. Every word hung like a gentle breeze drifting through an open window, stirring the questioning minds. I'm not sure how long I stood and preached. It could have been hours, or minutes. Who cared? Suddenly the altar was filled with weeping, and people rushing forward. How can I begin to relay with words what the Holy Spirit can accomplish when given the freedom to move in each life?

The following night herds of people converged on us. I preached on planting the Vision. "We need to invade all of these countries," I said with a fervor. "God has sent me with the Macedonian call, asking you to arise and shake this area for the Lord."

As I looked across the hungry faces intent on my every word, I could feel a great change taking place. It was as if they were ready to yield their lived back to A god that some of them had forgotten since childhood.

An unusually small child, a little girl, sat exceptionally close to her parent. The frail little hand clutched her mother's arm. Even from the pulpit I saw the eyes that stared from the emaciated body, racked by some dreaded disease. I began to pray for her even as my words continued.

"God has sent me back to stir up the gift of God that is within you," I said emphatically, using my hands to gesture to the center of my heart where the Holy Spirit does the work. "To stir it up," I said, "to stir it up," I enunciated again, "till we invade Albania, and Bulgaria, and Romania, and all of the Russian colonies for the Lord." I knew that God's Word was sharp and cutting and awakening sleeping hearts.

On the very front row, an old man, maybe in his late sixties, dropped his eyes. Possibly he was being reminded of the God he found in his youth. He wiped his eye.

"God wants Macedonians to rise up like Alexander the Great and go into all the world. 'Go,' He is saying. 'Go in the name of Jesus.'

"Evangelists not unlike myself are marching forward. No one knows the day or the hour of his return, but those called according to His purpose are excited and busy."

The crowd went away that night challenged, and the following day they were back again, seeking, being rekindled, and reawakened through the Holy Spirit flooding into this meeting.

On the last night of the meetings, I arrived early. I was heavily burdened. I felt a need to visit among the crowd, to get to know them. I needed to touch their spirit, for the sake of the Holy God of Abraham. My heart went out to these people. I had a love for them like I have never experienced before. As God was talking to them through me, their responses were ministering back to me. Minutes later when the crowd died down, a young man walked up to me.

"Thank you for coming to Greece," he said with a humble voice.

I found out later that he was the young teenager who had come to the front to shake my hand earlier. "I hear that you are a businessman. I want to have my own business when I finish school." He was trying to appear much more experienced than he was. He reminded me of a child, even though he was trying hard to look the part of a grown man.

"Seek God's wisdom to see this many people come out for preaching. They had their fairs and family gatherings, and once a week on Sunday a time of worship, which was created by their own imagination, but here I was talking about the God of creation, of the universe, as big as life itself, yet He was small and humble enough to come down and visit us in a personal way through the likeness of his son, Jesus Christ." My message went further. "That same God, so infinite and wise, gave up His son for you and me. What a mystery!"

The lights flickered. Maybe an angel of satan was walking about, looking to gain a foothold into a life.

That last night I preached on the sword, Jesus said, "I've not come to bring peace but to bring the sword." I took two characters, David and Balaam. "Many like Balaam are seeking rewards. But even though David did not seek a reward, he was a sinner. He committed murder and adultery. David paid for those sins, through that son Absalom, when he died by the sword."

Absalom usurped authority from David. "Yet David loved him so much, that he could not discipline him properly. Do you have a problem like that?" I asked. I felt a real burden for someone.

"This murderer. This man—who murdered men and children and shrunk their heads and hung them on his belt, and murdered Uriah and stole his wife—found favor with God. How could that be?"

You could have heard a pin drop. All ears were preened, every eye attached to mine. This was the Baltic area. Had they ever heard preaching like this?

"He repented..."

As I posed the statement, it was as if eyes could look inside their own heart, like a microscope bringing into focus with great clarity the tiny cells of a body. It is easy enough to see when something needs fixing, but it is not so easy to know how to fix your own.

"David cried out, 'Oh, Joab, don't kill my son, no matter what he has done, no matter if he has lain in wait to kill me, and went behind my back to wrestle my kingdom away from me. It was the ultimate picture of hatred, not the love of a son. Have mercy upon him.'"

I painted the picture for the audience of Joab, who as head of David's army was sworn to take care of David. His duty was to kill anyone or anything that jeopardized the King or his kingdom. Could Joab listen to the mumbling of a broken-hearten father over his runaway son?

Everyone there could hear and see the story inside their own lives, their own family secrets. It was almost unsettling, the quiet that settled across the audience.

I went on. "I couldn't help but think of some of the young men I see today with their manly comeliness, muscular frames, and long, flowing tresses." My voice fell an octave. "Which is a carbon copy of beautiful Absalom, David's handsome but rebellious son who got hung in the tree by his long, flowing locks.

"Joab made a decision David never could have. He ran and thrust Absalom through with the sword. God deals with sin just as Joab dealt with Absalom. But why did David escape with his life? He repented."

Chapter 31

Thousands Come To Riga, Latvia

During the same tour we were booked for a crusade in Latvia. Anatoly Sokalov, a minister of the Evangelical Baptist Church, met to welcome me and to spend some time in prayer before the crusades. He has a giving spirit, and I came to care deeply for the man. After seeing all the man does in the name of Jesus, I felt humbled. I deliberated over what I might do to show Sokalov I acknowledged his self-sacrificing service.

"Invite him to dinner," said Earnestine. "You know food is pretty scarce." It was an excellent idea, and I decided to ask Valentine, our driver, if he might like to accompany us.

The choice of eating places was not too numerous, but I believe we made the right one. "What would you like to eat?" I said, turning to Anatoly and then Valentine.

They eyed the menu. "I believe I will have..." said Anatoly. "I believe I will have whatever you have," he said ever so humbly, like he was used to accepting second best. I don't believe there is a haughty bone in his body. Valentine nodded the same.

I remember later, when Valentine drove us to Leningrad to a dollar store, Anatoly looked longingly at some sausage. He picked it up, looked at it, and after much thought, he lay it back down and picked up the smaller of the packages.

"No," I said. "We will take the larger package."

"Why is that?" he asked.

"Because it is the better buy," I said. I placed the smaller of the two back in the meat case. Tears filled his eyes as he was moved by my decision. When you live in America, with the cornucopia of plenty resting on every table, it is hard to understand how meagerly people in other countries are forced to live out their lives.

When the waitress came to our table, she nodded at me and smiled, giving me the opportunity to place our order.

"I believe we will have the Solanka Soup with fish broth," I said. "And we'll take it with capers, and a side order of vegetables." As an afterthought, just as she was about to exit the table, I added, "And bring us some beef stroganoff."

When I called to arrange for the table to be set aside, I requested that it be off by itself, and before dinner was served, Anatoly and I spent time in prayer for the crusade. We asked for the direct leadership of the Holy Spirit. I personally asked for strength to preach nothing but what God had for me to preach. In my spirit, I felt that God had great plans for these crusades.

From the time I first went to India, God opened my eyes to the needs around me. India was such a poor, under-developed nation. Riga and Latvia were not quite so comparable. In fact, they actually had little resemblance to India... except for one thing: their spiritual need. A soul without the spirit of God is barren and thirsty in any land.

The following day, I can't express what joy it was to see the crowds filing in through all corners of the stadium. Every night those crowds grew, as did the momentum of the sermons. One night the crowd was especially penitent. We sang songs and prayed, and I allowed the Holy Spirit to lead. The Spirit came like a sweet, sweet covering. Thousands were coming forward to give their life to Jesus. I saw weeping, and prayers being lifted up to a Holy God like I had never seen before. Suddenly it was as if God had stretched forth His hand across the audience. They began to stand up and come forward, one at a time, a caravan of contrite, weeping bodies filing forward for water that had the power to quench a lifetime of thirst.

"My daughter can see," cried a mother about her little eight-year-old. "She's been blind and now she can see!"

Another woman stood up and began walking briskly toward the

front. To most, it did not look like a miracle. To the lady, whose on leg had been extremely shorter than the other, it was a miracle. She almost ran the rest of the way down the aisle. She had limped through many years of life, now she was laughing and running and praising the Lord.

The sweet Spirit was leading, ministering, healing the deaf, the crippled, the dumb. A little deaf girl was hearing for the first time. She cried out, "Mama, Papa." A lady walked down the aisle. On her arm was an open sore that had been diagnosed as cancer. It disappeared instantaneously. Can I possibly say with human words like I just said and make you able to believe it in your heart? I don't know. All I know is that God was in that place. He heard the contrite and broken needy people as they cried out. Many hungry hearts were accepting Jesus Christ as their Savior. In the past, many years earlier, I had risked my life, not just once, but over and over, to preach here in Russia. Now the Russian government was asking me to come and preach the Gospel. What a miracle!

The KGB had brought corruption to their own people through the introduction of the Mafia. Jesus was bringing freedom through the blood of the cross. No longer would these daughters be encouraged to prostitute, or their sons to pimp. What the Mafia had given the blood of Jesus could wipe away.

The people cried in unison, cheering, saying, "Jesus is all!"

An older lady was given a New Testament. She was very sad because her husband was a drunkard, but she read St. John 1:12 and received Christ into her heart. She said, "I have never seen a book like this in all of my life."

For those who have been sheltered and given great opportunities, there is no way to begin to fathom the joy of freedom, freedom to have God's Word, and then the freedom to read the words He wrote. He wrote them to you and me personally! They're love letters. They tell us about God's love for us while we were yet in the darkness of our sin.

I stood looking out across the sea of faces remembering the Russian delegation that had come to Houston to invite me to come to Russia, to Moscow, to Leningrad, and to Kiev to hold crusades. Like an omen, I remembered with clarity the vision God had given me back in 1967. He'd said, "You will someday hold crusades in Russia." I had no idea back then. What a God, what a promise!

Chapter 32

George Bush and China

The doors were opening for me in China, but it didn't seem like they were opening fast enough. I was on another flight into China and it just happened that George Bush was scheduled to fly into Chendou, the capital city, at the same time. Chendou is an old city, famous for many things like Dung Xao Ping, who happened to be born there. Now it has grown into a metropolitan city with new hotels and shopping centers. The growth has expanded the economy and now the people have hope.

When I arrived the streets were blocked off in every direction for six blocks. The hotel security had arranged for the cordon because of the dignitaries.

"You can't go down there," they said.

"Well, I just flew in from Houston. I have standing reservations there," I shot back hurriedly.

"If you think you must go to that hotel, you will have to walk."

I thought on it a second and looked down at the large bags I had in my possession. Finally after much deliberation, I smiled and picked up my bags. I was glad I made a habit of carrying my own luggage. At least it kept me in shape. I must have looked like a sight in my western clothes. Here I went waddling down the street, half-carrying, half-dragging my bags. I guess I looked more like a panda bear. I had two large bags that were full of Bibles. They were heavy.

I made it down one block and took a breather. A couple of blocks later I pampered myself with another rest. I made it the next six blocks to a flight of stairs that formed a grand entrance into the hotel.

I can tell you, when I looked up at what must have been 100 steps—there may have been only fifty—there was no porter to help. I sucked in a gulp of air, picked up the bags and stepped to the first step.

"Who are you and what are you doing here?" asked an electrifying voice form the top of the stairs. A man in plain clothes was peering down his nose at me.

"I'm an American. I'm here on business. What in the world is going on?" My voice faltered from sheer exhaustion. I wasn't sure if I was being turned away or if I could take another tour.

"George Bush is here with Barbara."

"Wonderful. I'm from Houston, too. I can't believe this. Here I circle halfway around the world and run into a fellow Texan." I leaned over and rested my foot against the step. "That makes a good headline," I said laughing. "Chris Panos, minister, from Houston, Texas, traverses the world to meet the high dignitary from his own back yard."

"I'll tell him you're here," he said. "The press would probably like to see you." After a moment of silence he added, "I'm sure George would want to meet you. What did you say your name was?"

I laughed to myself, eyeing the long flight of steps, wondering if I had the stamina to make it. Minutes later, in the lobby of the hotel while I was checking in, I was having a hard time getting a room since all the rooms had been taken by the press and secret service men. Suddenly I heard a familiar voice. It was the security man I'd talked with earlier. He was passing through on his rounds.

"I talked to President Bush and Barbara," he said to me. "They said to tell you to come on in." He had a big grin. "After you get settled in, you are invited to their banquet room. They will be having dinner with the governor."

He breezed out as quickly as he had come. I checked in, showered, and put on my presentable clothes and walked into the banquet room with great interest. I knew a lot of the people. I had met the governor previously.

"Well, hello, Chris," George said, like he'd known me a lifetime. We talked, discussed the world situation, and had pictures made with each other. His cameraman did the honors. I was glad. I didn't even have a camera on me at the time. He said he'd send me one, which he did.

"Oh, I hear somebody from Texas," said the voice from behind me. "And I know that they are from Houston by their accent." Barbara Bush laughed and threw out her hand of friendship as she walked up.

We visited cordially, laughing over some Texas-size stories. There were many to share about Houston.

"Do you know George Mitchell?" I asked.

George Bush answered, "Yes," and then he laughed. "Yes, I've played tennis with him."

"He is Greek like myself," I said with a smile. One thing led to another. We talked of recent events in Houston. Barbara has a kind way about her, a Texas way of meeting people. George and I talked about China and how we might possibly reach them. By now he knew what my profession was. I learned over the years that no meeting is by chance. God has always made better introductions than I do.

They had just opened a second office in Schzeuwan, the western part of China. I was introduced as the first one to visit it.

"I'd like you to meet someone, Chris."

He quickly introduced me to a gentleman, a Chinese hotel man, who wanted to do great things. As soon as I saw the man, in my spirit, I knew why I was here.

God always gives me insight. Just by coincidence I had a gift for the man, as I usually did. It was an excellent way of opening doors. Usually the gift was a Bible or my book, *God's Spy*. When I know in advance who is on the agenda, the gift will have their name in gold, imprinted in the corner. Strangely enough, I thought of my book, and even the Bible, but instead I felt impressed to offer him something else: a simple piece of jewelry—a gold cross.

"Oh dear," he said. "Ordinarily I would not accept something like this, but I will accept this because my daughter is very religious."

My spirit knew this. "I have something she might like," I added, as I handed him a copy of *God's Spy*. "It's a copy of my book. I have a Bible for you and one for your daughter." It seemed the opportune time. God had opened doors on much less.

He thanked me, and he said, looking down at the cross, "God is my treasure. He has called me to China to share my treasure with you and your people."

Later, while I was visiting with Vice-President, George Bush, he introduced me to the governor. We got along well. Mr. Bush was a real nice person. I make it a point to know where I am going and to study about that country so I might be more prepared to minister. On many occasions I have read in the Bible where it tell us to "study to show thyself approved." Well, I studied many books, read their cold, dry facts about China, but when I began to walk among her people, I was touched to discover that they had a lot in common with me.

The Chinese value home and family and they enjoy life. I found a lot of laughter among the Chinese, much like my own heritage. To the Chinese, the family is an integral part of their life. Family ties run deep. They need that tie for financial and moral support. In my travels sometimes I would find as many as 200 people living together. It was strange. We Americans need space for security. The Chinese find security in togetherness.

"Mr. Panos, would you like to come to a party?" said a little old man I'd been introduced to. His grin filled his whole face. "At our party we will celebrate. It is a party set aside in honor of a name, so we call it name day."

I knew instantly what he was talking about. Other foreign countries celebrated NAME day, too. It's not much different than what we do here in America celebrating a birthday, or to celebrate events like Christmas when we honor Jesus Christ. The Russians set aside a "Chris" day, or a "George" day, or an "Anastasia" day, or a day set aside to honor or celebrate the person named.

This became a great witnessing tool for me in the Iron Curtain countries. It gave me the opportunity to visit intimately with people and tell them who I was named after, which opened the door for me to preach the Gospel, and the best part was the authorities had no idea Christ was even being considered. When new people I would meet invited me to a "Christos" day at their homes, it was the perfect introduction to share about my Lord, since the word Christos means Christ. I had already been involved with parties such as this in Albania and Romania. Now it was a nice introduction to China.

Chapter 33

Shanghai Communique

"China is closed," said many well-meaning Christians when they found that I was trying to break down the walls.

"Then why has God continued to burden me for her people and for all the places where lifting up the name of Jesus is an offense, punishable by imprisonment or sometimes death?" I would ask.

As I'd fly on another journey to smuggle in Bibles, I'd reflect on those statements and ask myself: Why was I doing this? Had my twenty years of Bible smuggling really made the difference? My years of hiding in the streets and delivering Bibles into Russia and China and other forbidden places? Had it really had any relation to change being seen?

I think so. Look at how the Berlin Wall fell down and Russia became a democracy. My heart was pricked for Russia, China, and India, but if I was listening to the world, the timing was never right.

"So, how much success can you have? Is it really worth taking the risks?" they'd ask cynically.

I came back with, "God leads, and those committed to His cause will follow."

That was the crux of questions rolling around in my head on that dark, lonely night when I was dining alone in a Shanghai restaurant. I wanted to touch something, wanted to hear a word from God on the plan for my life. I could tell anyone about the miracles. They were happening daily, but where did he want me to go now?

It was the middle of December, cold and lonely. It had been a hard week. China borders the southern part of Russia. My interest in the area encompassed all of the countries of the region. I'd spent time in crusades in India, not far away, just below the southwest providence of China, and I had been into Turkey, even as far as Hong Kong.

How could I forget the date? It was one of the coldest years on record. I had been smuggling Bibles for years, trying to get my foot in the door of China. Those who knew me and my business said I was seasoned. I knew the pros and cons of Bible smuggling, but even spiritual men get down. My sources provided me with many Bibles, so many that I had to extend my time there to get them dispensed. And there were obstacles to crawl over and through. Would I make home for Christmas? I do not think so. My thoughts were with Earnestine and the children.

The Shanghai restaurant was a little out-of-the-way place, a hole in the wall to some, but they served good food. Toward the front of the establishment, a young waiter was bussing tables, sporting a big grin. That smile lifted my spirits, capturing peace I was desiring at the moment.

"Tell me, young man, what is it that makes you smile so? I've been watching you as you set the tables. You've been smiling and conversing with people. I don't think you missed talking to one single person."

He looked surprised at my question. "Excuse me," he said. "Maybe I just like people." He had Asian jet black hair with brown eyes. He looked like a Christian. Maybe he knew the Lord and had acknowledged Him as savior. Could it be the Lord was preparing him to get saved?

I leaned over and dug into my briefcase to offer him one of my books. He thanked me, even before he looked to see what it was, bowed slightly, and said something in Chinese. A typical oriental gesture, but he did not look like a waiter. He could have been with secret Chinese police, and thoughts were racing through my mind.

"Thank you," he said again, looking like he was mulling over my question. He smiled as he looked down at the tittle.

"Do you read?" I asked.

"I am learning your language."

We talked further. I had the time to kill. He wasn't in a rush. The talk was informative for both of us. We discussed the weather and the events of the day that had been headline news.

"My father works for the daily newspaper," he said. "I get a lot of inside information before it gets to the papers."

We talked about his family, something he seemed very proud of. I'd dare to say he was more impressed with his family ties than most young Americans I chance to meet.

"Tell me," I asked. "Do you know who Jesus Christ is?"

He looked surprised, thought on it a minute, then said, "I am not sure. What company is that?"

How sad, I thought. This was not a trumped-up story. This young man the epitome of the great China following the death of Mao-Tse-Tung. I thought of the scope of what it was going to take to convert this world populous nation. It wasn't the time or place to deal with him about the subject, but I was sure God was not through with him. I decided to take a chance and lead him to Christ, and I began speaking about the Cross and the Blood of Jesus.

He said, "Jesus, dies for me?"

"Yes," I said, "Jesus went to the Cross and died for you that you might have everlasting life."

He looked straight into my eyes and said, "I accept Jesus Christ as my Lord and Savior."

A few years later I was back in Beijing, China, at Peking Square, only this time I was with Earnestine. We had our personal baggage chock full of New Testaments. It was a windy day. The sky had a sharp blue hue and was cloudless. It was early September. I was still trying my best to open doors. We had been delayed in our hotel room. Earnestine finally popped the question, "When are going to pass out these New Testaments?"

"When the timing is right," I said with anticipation.

"It's time," I said the next day about noon when we decided to take walk. I lugged the large overnight case of New Testaments down to Peking Square. Earnestine followed with her Polaroid camera. As soon as we emerged at Mao's tomb, she began taking pictures that were being developed on the spot. These Chinese had never seen a camera that made instant pictures. They got exited and that drew a crowd of people. I opened the suitcase and told Earnestine to start passing out New Testaments and the chocolates.

People came from everywhere. Earnestine's face was blushing as the sun sparkled down on her cheeks. The Chinese had such innocent faces as they swarmed Earnestine and me. It was incredible to see the God of old working salvation in China. "Except the Father Spirit draw them they will not come." They came by the dozens, and also the secret police cometh. The people formed a tight circle around us. They were protecting us form the police. It is written that God is our Shield, Praise His Holy Name. Earnestine handed a New Testament and some chocolate to one policeman; he looked and he looked, and then he said, "Che, Che, yes, yes, thank you." Wow. What a miracle-working God we serve. Now our contraband New Testaments had been delivered.

Chapter 34

A Bolt of Lightning

It was a few minutes later, with more Bibles to deliver in Beijing and out of sheer frustration from repeated failures, that I decided to try something new and innovative. "Self," I said. "God is innovative. You need to be, too."

The cab driver who had driven me around town for nearly an hour turned to me rather skeptically. "Do you have a purpose in driving around in circles?" He looked passively concerned. "I do not mind as long as you are watching the meter."

Suddenly as if a bolt of lightning had been thrust down from heaven, I leaned forward in the seat. "Would you mind stopping the car and climbing up on the roof?"

He glared back at me like I was mad. "Stop the car and climb on the roof?" His forehead creased.

"Yes, I'll do the talking. You do the translating."

After a moment's hesitation, he said sarcastically, "What's in it for me?"

I could tell his English was broken and his clothing was good for a foreigner. I guess you could say he was a "dapper Dan" in his country. He said, "I know economics and how democracy works." I told him to stop the car immediately. I felt the urgency of the Spirit to jump on the hood of the car, and using it as a platform and a podium, just as suddenly I began passing out Bibles and some chocolates and bubble gum that I had brought along with me. They swarmed on me. Everyone wanted what I had in my big brown bag. Within ten minutes we had distributed the entire case of Bibles. I thank God for such an opportunity, and it reminded me of a mini open-air crusade as I preached Christ to them. They walked off smiling, some holding their little books to their heart as if it were the most precious possession they had ever had. I noticed others looked at their New Testament as if they had never seen anything like it before. Over the years I have felt a little likeness to James Bond, especially when I would have a close call. I recall an incident in Moscow at the beginning of my ministry smuggling Bibles behind the Iron Curtain. It was 1960 and it was a cold day in December, snow falling over the cathedrals as I tramped down the streets leaving footprints in the snow. Then the Lord spoke to me, "Son, if you follow my footprints I will lead you like you have never been led before. Do not be afraid, for I am with you and I will never leave you or forsake you."

I marched into the Metropole Hotel, and I walked up a beautiful staircase that needed a touch-up of paint. It reminded me of Tara from the movie *Gone With The Wind*. As I proceeded up the second floor, I went directly to the American Express office, and there I met a young lady who introduced herself as Sonya. I asked her could she change some dollars into rupees and that I also needed to cash a check.

Sonya said, "Yes," and then it seemed to me that she was taking a deep interest in me and I later could understand why.

I felt an unction to speak to her about communion that is offered in the Greek and Russian Orthodox Church. I told her that in the communion, the wine stood for the blood of Jesus Christ. That every time we partook of communion it was in remembrance that Jesus spilled his blood at Calvary. I said to Sonya, "Can you see Him on the cross? Can you see His nail-scarred hands? Can you see the wound in His side? Can you see the blood coming out of that wound? Can you see His bleeding stripes?" I noticed that tears began to stream down her cheeks and she lost her composure and began to just cry and cry. I said, "Sonya, you have such a tender heart and I know you love God. Have you ever asked Jesus to come into your heart? Have you ever done this?"

She said, "No, but I want to."

I said, "Repeat this after me. Dear Jesus, come into my heart. Please come into my heart. I accept You as my Lord and Savior."

I was astonished then as she began to reveal to me about how the KGB worked. She said, "Watch out for the one-two punch that you Americans express in the U.S.A. We Russians detest and deplore all American dogs. We are trained this way. One way is that we capture pictures by a hidden camera placed in the wall behind a picture in the frame and it is focused on the bed. We conveniently place a beautiful, young lady there and when that American congressman or that businessman V.I.P. takes the bait, we then have captured his picture. We can decide in the future to blackmail him with his government or his family into telling us secret information about the plans that the United States has toward Russia. If this doesn't work, we then use greed by offering a hundred-to-one exchange of money. Sometimes we catch ambassadors, congressmen, even Secretary of States."

Then my mind drifted back to China and how it didn't take long for me to run into China's underground network of agents. They were counterfeits fashioned for the KGB. My experience with the Chinese leaders was different though. I approached one of the Chinese leaders. "Why is it," I said, "that in Russia God just does not exist?"

"They don't want their people to hear about it for fear it might become important to them."

"But you people of China do not feel the same?"

"In China we don't fear God or the church. It's more like we see no reason to endorse it," he said, yawning.

The Chinese people had some very redeeming qualities. I'll never forget the very first day I flew into China. I stood waiting at the baggage checkout. "What are you waiting for?" asked the airport employee.

"I'm waiting for my luggage." I showed him my baggage stubs, and he wrote the numbers down. I had no idea why.

"Where will you be staying?" he asked.

I told him.

"Your luggage will be brought over to the hotel for you shortly," he said with a smile.

With much reluctance, I walked off. I had no proof I would ever see my bags again. A couple hours later they arrived, unhampered with the Bibles still intact. China wasn't forbidding Bibles or Christianity. They thought of it as just another opium, something to quiet their sleeping nation. That is, as long as it did not get a real foothold and their people did not take it seriously.

Chapter 35

The Chinese Secret Police

As God opened doors for me in China, I accepted them with great enthusiasm. I thought from past trials in other countries that China would not be an easy country to penetrate, but at least it was not like Russia. I thought I wouldn't have the KGB to contend with. I was mistaken.

It was close to 9:30 p.m. when I made my way to the dining room of the Beijing Hotel. The restaurant was jam packed, wall to wall with people. I couldn't help think how beautiful the lobby was. You could look up to the ceiling and see one the prettiest atriums I guess I had ever seen. The lobby had a Chinese restaurant and the decor was modern. It was with a little red gate in front of the restaurant. The red gate stands for happiness in Chinese. The waiter appeared and handed me a menu, and as I looked it over, it was superb.

Then the waiter suggested, "Try the western lobster tail and steak over a bed of rice."

I looked down at the marble floors that were black and white. I was amazed to see on the menu that they had T-bone steaks from Texas. I said to myself laughingly, "I bet it's Mongolian beef from Mongolia," and I asked the waiter and he said, "Oh, no sir we fly it in from Texas weekly" and then from the roar of languages, they appeared to be having a contest over who could be heard above the other. I followed the maitre d' to the table in the corner. I dug into my coat pocket for a business card.

"Please take this," I said handing him the card. "When a tall gentleman with a shock of white hair comes in and asks for me, direct him to my table."

He flashed a broad smile and disappeared.

The man I was supposed to meet had agreed to meet early. With a great desire on my part, and through a joint effort of many people involved, I had entered a business deal for the printing of the New Testament in Mao's language. There was open criticism. Of course, there was often open criticism of my outreach. This time I was told that we Bible smugglers were using "clandestine techniques." I knew better. In the past, in many Communist countries, the legal Bibles were only distributed to churches that adhered to the Communist government, and even then they had to show that they would not cause trouble for the party. I soon learned that many of the evangelical Protestants in China would have had nothing to teach and share from had it not been for the smuggled Bibles and the people who risked everything to smuggle them.

I sipped my coffee and flipped through some paperwork as I waited. I thought of a recent conversation I'd had with a mainlander. "To survive you must adapt." This particular author had no claim to fame, no real success story, but he had lived long enough to gain wisdom. Every day in my struggle to carry the Bible I was learning to adapt; to try new methods of delivery.

"I bring him to you," said the little man as he approached with the tall white-headed gentleman.

I rose to my feet and graciously thanked the maitre'd before I dismissed him. I turned to take the gentleman's hand. "Mr. Tung?" I said with a smile.

"Yes," he said as he seated himself.

Since I had not yet asked him to do so, I found it striking, and as unique to his culture as his stature. He was the first tall oriental I had ever met. Our first meeting, even though we shared common goals and contacts, seemed a little guarded.

"Where are you from?" I asked, trying to break the ice.

"From Shanghai."

I smiled. "I've visited your area. It has a great market place, many bargains..."

He didn't wait for me to finish; instead he bounded into conversation. "One preacher, a Baptist minister, has come under sharp investigation by the government. They have done everything they can to scatter his congregation. He had about 300 members when he was arrested and jailed."

"What was his offense?"

"He wouldn't sign up to pay allegiance to the Communist government. I have friends who have signed up, and they now have very limited freedom to preach. Mr. Panos, there is a Chinese KGB just as there is one in Russia. The operative officer comes and sits in the services and shuts it down if the words are not what he thinks the government wants to hear."

I was thoroughly familiar with Russia's KGB, of course; I had only been recently introduced to the Chinese version. "What would you have me do for you, Mr. Tung?"

"We need Bibles and volunteers to help set up training. We need your years of experience in dealing with the KGB."

"China needs a national church, Mr. Tung. Only about 3 million people have become Christians, and those are scattered and detached from any mainline group. You need a method of pulling yourself together."

"It will not happen. The government would look on that as anti-government."

"Let us pray for this cause, Mr. Tung. And when we are through, give me time to think on it. Possibly I might be able to help further."

We bowed our heads and said a meaningful prayer. Then we spent the remainder of an hour discussing ways we could work together to bring union from discord. China, on the surface, was closed to the spreading of the Gospel. But in my heart I felt it was time for a spiritual breakthrough.

When Mr. Tung said his goodbye, I decided to take a walk. I was walking along thinking of Mr. Tung and his dilemma and wondering why God had brought him my way. At the present, I wasn't sure what I could do to help. I liked the sights and sounds of Hong Kong. Sometimes I would sit and listen and appreciate the fact that I had the power and freedom to come and go, which was more than most of these people had. I sat watching people, turning my thoughts toward my own home and friends which reminded me of an earlier trip to Hong Kong.

A few months earlier, I had arrived in Hong Kong tired and weary. It had been a time of deliberation for me as it was now. I was staying on the Kowloon side. I crossed the street and went into the Peninsula Hotel. For some unfathomable reason I decided to go up to the mezzanine floor. I was walking and daydreaming, thinking about Earnestine and the children. I stopped at a jewelry store to admire a piece of fine jewelry. Suddenly I saw a reflection of someone in the window. I stepped aside and made my way around the corner. "God loves you, and the best is yet to come!" I said with a deep, resonant voice to the person with their back to me.

"Oh, dear. That must be Chris Panos," said the lady as she whirled around. It was Debra Paget, the movie star, a long-time friend of Earnestine's. Many of you may remember her in the famous Biblical movie *The Ten Commandments* starring Charlton Heston. When she turned around she was smiling. "I knew it was you." She threw out her arms and hugged me.

Debra had been a dear friend of Earnestine's for a long time. Many who know her are not aware that she is related to royalty. She is the niece by marriage to Madam Chaing Kai-shek, the wife of the past leader Chiang Kai-shek, of China. After years being our friend, we came to think of her as a princess among women and a spiritual sister to Earnestine. I wondered why she came my way this day.

"Where are you staying?" she asked.

"Over at the Sheraton," I answered.

"Yes, I have business there."

She and I spent the next couple of hours praying and shopping, since I knew some outlets in Hong Kong. I had to cut my time short since I had a plane flight out early that afternoon to Shanghai.

Daydreams and memories were always refreshing, especially when one was so far away from home, but suddenly I was back on track, and just as perplexed as ever over the situation. It was time for prayer and fasting. My years of traveling the length and breadth of China made me cry for her bondage. How do you look at the millions of people, far more than the population of America, all clustered in overcrowding yet totally bereft of God and His principles? I felt in my heart that China was ready for change, but back-up funds were needed to do solid work there.

At that time China was not forbidding Bibles or Christianity, but they thought of it as just another opium, something to quiet their sleeping national. They would tolerate it as long as it did not get a real foothold, and as long as their people did not take it too seriously.

One night at a dinner for one of their leaders, a friend asked, "What are the two most important subjects in America?" Before I could answer, he went on. "In China it is science and engineering, the two most highly-acclaimed professions to enter." He looked proud of his statement. "And we have perfected the technology for spying from satellite."

I laughed out loud. "And we Americans have gleaned information from your efforts for years. We have even duplicated your devices," I said. I thought about the scanner attached to my telephone. I laughed again thinking to myself that I was the rebuttal to their KGB. Many wondered where my allegiance lay. Chris Panos, Double Agent... or was it Triple Agent?

Chapter 36

The Embassy Makes House Calls

As I began to travel extensively into China, I realized something few ever do. There really are two Chinas. Not Taiwan and the mainland like most think, but rather the image we have of China and the reality of China. The most surprising of all things, after my travels there I learned the Embassy makes house calls. The China that we have known is National China. The China that President Chaing Kai Shek ran with an iron hand. But after the overthrow of Chaing Kai Shek, China became Red China. Mao Tse Tung and his promotor, Lin Pao, created the little red book. For many of you that don't understand what the little red book was, it was a red Bible promoting Mao as a Chinese god. This little red book was used to brainwash one-third of mankind. Think about that. One out of every three people that walked down the street is Chinese. Mao and Lin Pao's little red book was responsible for purging and killing millions of Chinese. He caused his China to be directed until it began to worship him as a god. The little red book was designed after the Bible and quotes many of the verses being changed to fit Mao's personality. Let me given you an example of what the little red book accomplished. In 1968 they started the campaign of the hidden brother. The hidden brother concept wrecked China, and an example is a carpet company that had twenty-five employees, and every person at work had to report to his supervisor what happened during that day. This was used for the purpose of gathering information to see if people were speaking well of Mao. At home the children would hear all about what was being said in the family. They were required to tell the school teacher everything their parents had said that night. This injected a fear in China to such an extent that no one hardly spoke to one another. It was a crucial and sobering time. All freedom of speech was lost. If they were negative toward Mao, they would be arrested, thrown in jail and eventually hung.

The sun was just rising over Hong Kong harbor that bright June morning as my taxi pulled up at the Kowloon railroad station. For years I had looked at this building the way a discontented East German would look at the Brandenbury Gate in Berlin. This day was different. This day I had a Chinese visa in my pocket and a train ticket to Canton. I was exuberant.

I climbed aboard the antiquated train and seated myself. The train reminded me of a conveyor belt, rolling along, not just the ninety miles to Canton, but the trip from one universe to another. The passengers were a mixture of classes: housewives, workmen, and many students all heading for the New Territories. To the right of me and forward a few rows sat a covey of young people. The reference was fitting. Young people getting together to produce a language equal to the sound of a dove's coo. From the way they were dressed, I assumed they might be going to Shatin for a swim. The train was their "local" subway ride to Manhattan.

Turning sideways, I introduced myself to the little Chinese fellow with the strange-looking hat sitting right next to me. I was not ignorant, but I wasn't sure what providence this man came from.

"Good morning!" I bowed. "I'm Chris Panos."

"Good morning to you," he said in broken English as he bowed slightly. His English was far from distinguishable, yet I think his attempts at English would have been much more understandable than I would have been in his language. We tried to make small talk.

The train lumbered along the tracks, and for a brief moment I felt like a baby rocked in a cradle. As we approached the border village of Lo Wu, I could see the peasants in their broad hats carrying big packages. It was a peaceful scene. A chicken scratched placidly at the door of a banyan tree.

"Where are you headed?" said the gentleman seated to the other side of me who had overheard my introduction to the little man.

"I am here to see your country. I'm a businessman from America," I said enthusiastically. "What is your profession?"

"I'm a politician from Komeito, Japan."

I smiled and extended my hand. "I have never been to your city," I said apologetically.

"That's okay. I have never been to America either."

We both laughed.

"This must be an international train?" I said, looking around.

"It appears to be. The gentleman ahead of you is an Indian diplomat. I see him often. I always feel a certain excitement when I ride into Canton."

"Do you go there often?"

"I used to." He looked pensive. "On the Chinese side, in the township of Shumchun, the color of red jumps out like a carnival."

"When I entered the country, my luggage was not even examined. I've been through customs in almost every country, but your border officials seemed hardly interested. That's a change."

"China is changing, but isn't every place?"

He gave a valid point. We talked off and on for the duration of the ride. He was well-educated and especially interesting to visit with. God kept nudging me. I pulled out a small testament just as we were leaving the train for the stop over and offered it to him.

"Oh," he said when he saw what is was, "no, thank you." His words were kind. "Actually I have no need of it." He paused a minute, as if debating over it, then reached over and accepted it. "Maybe I will take it. It will be a reminder to me of the train ride into Canton." He flashed a winning smile.

I prayed God's blessing on the man as I walked off.

The hotel lobby gave way to a whitewashed balcony all covered with grapevines. Through the brilliance of the green leaves, I could see the red soil and curved hills of Kwangtung. In the foreground were two huge signboards. They were red and white with political exhortations. In my earlier visits, Mao's picture adorned the interior and exterior of buildings, much like Jesus' picture adorns a church.

I had been on the train for some time, and now I felt as if I had a hole in my stomach, and I decided it was time to eat. I noticed a woman called Miss Wong and she was talking to another guest on the train. I had overheard her previously speaking to another passenger and I knew that she was very knowledgeable of President Nixon's visit to China, and I believe she was an agent or worked for the railroad in some police capacity. I straightened my tie and headed toward the dining room. Just as I reached the broad marble stairway, two maids emerged from the laundry room carrying towels and bedding. "Am I too late for breakfast?" I asked as I hurried by.

"Oh no. It is still being served, but if you happen to miss it, we would be glad to open the kitchen to you," they called after me.

A few minutes later, Miss Wong walked by and asked me if she could escort me to the dining room. I spoke small talk. She kept bringing up the name of President Richard Nixon. I recalled the many trips President Nixon had made into China. From her questions I assumed she knew a little about our country.

"I think Canton is too hot," she said as she waited for me to be seated.

I laughed and nodded in agreement. She was very engaging. It was a refreshing change. The last time I had been here it was much more disciplined.

Across the brightly-lit dining room, I could see the Komeito party of politicians again. The Indian diplomat was only two tables away. The Komeito politicians had their carry-on luggage sitting in the floor beside them. I was barely into my meal when a whistle pierced the calm. The train for Canton was ready to go. I stuck an item or two into my pocket and ran out behind the group.

Back in 1964 I had ridden this train in the reverse direction. Riding it again made me realize the great changes that had taken place. Not just in China herself, but in her relationship to the world. I pondered her new importance as the train sped across the East River and on to Canton. After years of traveling, I discovered the real vehicle for traveling into China is not the plane or a train. It's a piece of paper three inches by five, elegantly printed in red and black ink, with headings of "entry or exit visa." In 1964 my visa had been issued in Poland. It was the end of summer. I applied for a Chinese visa in London and Paris and was turned down. Then I tried again in Moscow, and again I was turned down. Once inside Budapest I tried again, and finally Prague. The response was not "yes," but it was not a flat "no" either. I was very frustrated, and I finally reached Warsaw, my last port call in Europe before returning to Houston. I went to the Chinese Embassy, the fawn oblong block building on Bonifraterska Street. I had barely a flicker of hope when I asked to see the Ambassador. Possibly I wanted to complain, but more than anything I wanted to make my plea.

"What may I help you with?" he asked rather coolly.

"I want a visa to go into China."

He looked surprised.

My plea was seriously received. A senior Chinese diplomat sipped his tea as I made my pitch. I talked about my interest in China and told them about me being a businessman. It was a good visit. At least for the first time I was allowed to discuss reasons.

"You make a convincing statement," said the official after hearing my reasons for wanting to go to China. Shortly afterward, I was ushered out into the marble lobby.

"Thank you for coming. We will call you."

I laughed and said to myself, "Sure you'll call everyone at home and tell them their visa is in."

Oh well. I did my best. I went home and retired for the evening.

At eleven o'clock I was in bed asleep at the Hotel Bristol when the phone rang. It struck fear; I hated late-night callers.

"Hello," I said sleepily. I had no idea who would be calling at this time.

The voice cracked through the dark of the night. "Your visa has been okayed, Mr. Panos. You may pick it up it up at the Chinese Embassy tomorrow morning at eight."

"Thank you," I stammered, half-asleep, finding it unbelievable that I actually did receive a call. It certainly wasn't the norm; then again, I had been traveling for so long, for so many years, and in so many different countries. I doubted there was a norm anymore. The best part of this story was that amidst the diplomatic fluidity of the spring of 1964, the Chinese Embassy in Warsaw stamped the visa in the passport. A few years later, in 1971 when I once again tried to apply to go to China, I learned the officials said simply, "The visa will not be stamped into your passport, the comrades in Warsaw made a mistake in doing that back in 1964." I laughed to myself. All the other doors for me to enter China had been slammed shut. That mistake opened the doors. I realized that when God opens a door, He does it however He chooses to accomplish it.

Chapter 37

Divine Appointment

It was past midnight when I flew into Hong Kong on a Boeing 707 jet. Now I sat in the darkened house praying for God's direction. Across the room, a huge old Chinese desk sat observing my actions. When feeling apprehensive, my first remedy is to pray—prayers like the ones my mother offered up to an almighty God for me. I didn't know what God was about to accomplish, but I knew I was here as a sovereign act of God.

I stood at the window reminiscing of the past times I'd spent in Hong Kong. Suddenly a vision came. My visions were as real as life. I saw the Kowloon side of Hong Kong. I was walking down the street admiring the color and the pomp and suddenly ran into Glen Ewing, his wife, and his daughter Edna Locker, all dear friends of mine. The vision was so real I felt I could have reached out and touched them. For some reason their image was very strong in my mind's eye. I shook my head, realizing it was a dream. I was let down and troubled over the vision and unsure what it meant.

In the shadow of the curtain, I slid open the window where the air was mild with coming summer. A hint of jasmine floated upward from the gardens below. I thought back a previous trip into the area. When my plane landed in Tokyo, I went into the airport, where I browsed the postcard section of the gift store. I felt strangely detached, even lonesome, and purposely chose a card for Earnestine. If she were here with me right now, I would be able to share with her the vision I had just had.

"Mr. Panos?" said a voice through the door. I whirled around.

The voice may have been calling out my name before I heard him. A bellhop stood smiling at me, holding out a piece of luggage. "I believe this is yours."

"Oh," I said eagerly. "Yes. Put it down over there." I pointed to an open space below the ornately carved picture frame.

I paid him and closed the door, still thinking about the dream. I retired early and had fitful night's sleep. The next morning I headed to the China Travel Service. En route I had to pass by many shops. My, what a fever to sell as they hawked expensive clothes and watches at incredible prices. Usually a sucker for a bargain, I'd stop and listen and often buy, but this day I walked right on past. Up on the second floor of the China Travel Service, I stopped at the counter. The people were curt, void of any friendliness.

"May we help you?" the man asked. I have to admit his somber face dampened my spirit. Americans were considered imperialists at that time.

"I need a visa to visit the Mainland of China."

"What nationality are you?" he asked, as if he didn't know.

"I am Greek American. You must give me a visa."

He didn't smile or reply as he walked off. As I waited, I noticed on the wall across the hall nasty words had been hastily scribbled condemning the Yankee Imperialist. The man obliged me in my request, but not because he wanted to.

As I was leaving the Travel Service, my plans were to take the ferry across the harbor to Hong Kong Island. I was still remembering my vision earlier. I didn't make it two blocks down the street and suddenly I had a vision again of Rev. Glenn Ewing, his wife, and daughter. But this time it was so real I shouted out his name without thinking.

"Look! It's Chris Panos," shouted Edna Locker.

I ran across the street and embraced them and shook their hands, elated that it wasn't a vision. I rejoiced thinking how God brought about such special divine appointments. I shared with them my vision the previous day and we all rejoiced.

"Think about this," I said. "God brought each of us out of the

Y.M.C.A. Hotel, where we were staying, at just the right time."

Brother Ewing smiled.

"Let's go over to the Peninsula Hotel and have some tea," I said. "When did you arrive?" I asked.

"We arrived here from Formosa only yesterday."

Here we had to traveled 15,000 miles from Texas to meet suddenly by God's special appointment. God must have known I needed spiritual support that day. After we prayed, we went to see the amazing city of Hong Kong and Ceylon together.

"Brother Ewing, I have a great desire for China, and I am here because I believed God is about to open doors for me."

The following day we spent the time in prayer and fasting. It was an emotional time.

God was very close. I had an anointed shout of praise in my being. Not a forced chorus of praise, but one that came from the study of the Scripture. It affirmed many things daily for me as I read the Scripture. This praise went beyond the beauty of the sunrise or awesomeness of the sunset. It gave newness of life.

At the close of those three days it seemed God was saying, "the time is right" to reach China. He told me, "Businessmen will come to China, even our President Nixon." In 1968, that was out of the question, totally ludicrous. In 1970 I sent President Nixon my book, *He Called, I Followed*. On the front cover it showed a picture of the Bible in my fist breaking through the Bamboo Curtain. He wrote a letter and thanked me for my book. Soon after that, President Nixon made his decision to go to Red China.

A few days later and early in the morning, when I got to the Y.M.C.A., the Holy Spirit led me inside to see Brother Ewing again. We met in the chapel for prayer. As we left the area and stepped out across the street, Brother Ewing turned to me.

"God is impressing me to tell you something, Chris. Please do not be offended. My message to you is: 'The timing is right for China, but the conditions are not right, at least not yet. Thousands will be killed and the leaders will be shaken up.'"

Brother Ewing thought that Mao would be killed. His words came to pass, but instead of Mao, it was Lin Pao who was done away with. China was thrown into a panic as Lin Pao tried to escape into Russia, and his plane crashed. The Culture Revolution was killing Chinese left and right, and China could have collapsed. The man that turned it around was the cool-headed Chou En Lai. He moved quickly and began to restore order throughout China.

I stared at him with a startled expression. I felt so impressed that it was the perfect time. Why would he say this to me? "Thank you, Brother Ewing," I said with gentleness of spirit, "but I will have to pray about this word you have given to me." I had not fully divulged what God had been impressing on me. Many times in my ministry, I have felt impressed about something. I usually go with those gut feelings, but because the respect I had for Bro. Glenn Ewing, I wondered if by some mighty miracle the Lord had set an appointment in Hong Kong for me to run into Brother Ewing in order to redirect my path.

I chose to follow Brother Ewing's direction. And a few days later, the very same time I would have arrived in Canton, hundreds of Chinese were machine-gunned down at the train station. I was so very glad to learn an important lesson walking with the Almighty at my side. What a mighty God we serve.

God is my provider, and the Lord directs me through many ways. I left thanking God.

Chapter 38

Angels

Whether I was in Russia, India, China, or a host of other forbidden countries, there were times I would find myself in fearful situations. I knew my strength came from God.

Hadn't He been faithfully providing miracle after miracle? Yet being human I'd sometimes forget and get caught up in doing it on my own. God began to show mysteries and that he was dispensing His Holy Angels to protect me. On more than one occasion one of those angels helped save my life.

It was almost dusk as I waited in the bookstore looking out the window at the bustling street. I was on New Jerusalem Street, a street in Warsaw, Poland. I had been smuggling Bibles into the country for months. For days I'd been in this bookstore off and on, watching and waiting for my contact. The game of "hurry up and wait" is boring enough, so I decided to try and see if I could distinguish which prospective book customer would be my next contact. For days I had been cautiously dealing with one man who had put forth great effort to answer all my questions, even mentioning Cathleen Gabon, a close mutual friend of ours, or so he said. But I had stumbled onto some information that I was not dealing with one person, but a group of people. It was enough to make me want to break and run. The evening before the group of people had agreed to meet at my hotel at 8 p.m.

The minute they walked through the door, I counted the heads of seven seemingly cautious pedestrians who were definitely apprehensive. For reasons beyond understanding, their interpreter did not show. I was required to make a quick decision to attain one, so I looked around. I'd been in traps before. I approached the desk clerk. "Would you mind coming over and helping?" I asked. "I need someone to translate?"

He looked friendly, about the only friendly face around. "On one condition," he said. "We all must agree to be careful what we say." His words dropped like a child's whisper. I nodded, agreeing. We were seated and about ready to begin when a dark-haired gentleman came bursting through the large double doors, looking around like he had a reason for being there. "Excuse me," he said very matter-of-factly. "I'm sorry I am late. I'm the interpreter." He was the kind of personality that took control. The group nodded in agreement and began asking questions. I wasn't even sure where the other man disappeared.

"Why are you willing to smuggle Bibles into Communist countries?" they asked me pointedly. "Who are your contacts? Have you never been taken to jail for this?"

It was supposed to be an interview by people who were in the same shoes as me, but their questions made me feel like I was being scrutinized rather than interviewed. I grew silent, feeling jumpy with no clear witness in my spirit about these people. Usually when I share with "godly" people who are working for the underground, I feel a real defining of values as well as a meshing if my own. At the close of the meeting, we agreed to come together the following night at the hotel at eight p.m.

Even before the last person was gone, the clerk who I had talked to earlier was motioning for me, trying to get my attention. "Don't go to that meeting," he said under his breath.

"Why would you say that?" I had all the intentions of going, but I was waiting to hear his answer.

He took on a somber expression. "They are going to tape your conversation for evidence. You will be arrested. They will put you into jail. I am here to tell you to get out of the city as quickly as you can."

His words were piercing. Here I was in Poland. Earnestine and the kids were happily waiting my return at home. I was already questioning my contacts. I said a quick goodbye and went back to my room to pray.

I paced the floor, thinking what to do. I wasn't sure how I was supposed to respond to his statement. I opened my Bible and began to read. Suddenly my eyes dropped down to the passage in Acts 22: 18-19:

"Make haste, and get thee out of Jerusalem; for they will not receive the testimony concerning you."

That was my answer, I was sure of it, but to verify it I jumped to my feet and went down to the lobby. I needed to talk with the desk clerk again. Maybe he knew something more about the group of people than I did. He was nowhere to be found. I walked the length and breadth of the hotel trying to find him. After a few minutes I stopped at the front desk.

"I'm sorry to bother you, but where is the other desk clerk, the one that was on duty last night?"

The man looked at me like I was crazy. "I'm sorry, I don't know what you are talking about."

I thought it was sort of joke, but the look on his face told me otherwise. "He is about five foot nine with dark hair and brown eyes," I said, using my hands to talk with. "He had a slight scar above his above his left eyebrow."

"There is no one here like that," he said.

"Didn't you see the group of men sitting over there tonight at about eight p.m.?"

"Yes." He looked at me like I was strange."

"Remember I walked over here and got the desk clerk. He went back with me to help translate the meeting."

"That's impossible," he said with raised brows. "There are no other employees on this shift, and I certainly did not go over there." He didn't give me time to ask further but walked off, shaking his head.

Who was the clerk, and why was he there at just the right time? I didn't know the answer to those questions, but I did as I was instructed. I left the area.

A year later when I was back ministering to the underground churches there in Warsaw, they told me that many Christians had been arrested by that same group, and that they found out later that they were Communists spies. In my hour of need, God sent a way for my narrow escape from Poland.

Was this just a coincidence? I don't think so. That wasn't my only heavenly visitation.

God sent me to Korea and India, where he graciously granted miracles of salvation and healing. When the newspaper got wind of the meetings there in Caddappa, India, they sent reporters from *The Daccan Chronicle*, *The Hindu*, and *The Indian Express*; all of them wanted an interview to discredit this thing about miracles.

"How are these miracles taking place?" they asked.

Before I could answer, the reporters had their own preconceived answer. I'm not sure why they bothered to interview me. They had all the answers. Suddenly out of nowhere, seven insane demon-possessed women broke through the crowd. They were screaming and flailing themselves, trying to wreck havoc with God's crusade.

I moved on my first response after having experienced this kind of demonstration before, and I stood up and lifted my hand out to them. "I command you, in the Name of Jesus, fall to the ground." As if I was performing magic, they fell to the ground like dead people. They then began to lay perfectly still. I led the crowd in the sinners' prayer.

"Rise up and be whole," I said. They stood to their feet and began professing Jesus Christ. They testified later in front of the crowd their deliverance. Believe me, when God first began to move in my crusades like this, I was in as much wonder as you. I continued to preach Jesus Christ and his salvation, and He continued to perform His miracles.

For those of you who have never been to a crusade out in the wilderness, you could in no way be prepared for events such as this. The reporters came to scoff, but they went away believers. The bystanders came to leer, but they saw with amazement the miracles.

God takes a negative and makes it into a positive.

Who was the desk clerk that warned me to flee from Poland? Was it a ministering angel sent from heaven to protect me? What angel was there when I commanded in Jesus' Name the demons to loose the woman in India? Billy Graham has aptly described the angels as "God Secret Agents." ("Holy, Holy, Holy is the Lord of Hosts, the whole earth is full of His Glory!") Psalms 103: 20-21; Isaiah 6: 1-3; Revelation 5: 6-14; 7: 9-12; 8: 1-4; 11: 15-19. The angels are avid observers of events on earth. They rejoice in celebration as the mighty deeds of God unfold and the plan of salvation is accomplished. Each sinner's repentance is the cause of great happiness among the hosts of angels. Job 38: 7; Luke 15: 7-10; Hebrews 12: 22. God uses His angels to guard, protect, and guide His people. Genesis 24: 7-40; Exodus 33: 2; II Kings 6: 8-23; Psalm 34: 7; 91: 11; Daniel 3: 28; 6: 22; 12: 1; Acts 12: 11. The concept that everyone has a personal guardian angel is a time-honored and widespread conviction among Christians. Biblical support for this idea is found in Matthew 18: 10 where Jesus says, "See that you do not look down on one of these little ones. For I tell you that their ANGELS in heaven always see the face of my Father in heaven." Some have suggested on the basis of Acts 12: 15 that a guarding angel takes on the appearance of the mortal to whom he is assigned. The angel of the Lord went to the prison to release Peter the Apostle. His chains fell off and the gate opened of its own accord. Then Peter or His angel was knocking at the door were the saints of God where praying for Peter. "I remember one time when I was preaching in India, someone said I saw you at Athens, Greece, at the airport. 'Chris,' I yelled at the top of my voice. I guess you were in a hurry then, as suddenly you vanished?" Have you seen someone you know somewhere and this person simply just disappears? This has happened to many Christians. A belief in the ministry of guardian angels was also widespread in Judaism. And Moses said, "He sets the bounds of the nations according to the number of the angels of God" (Deuteronomy 32: 8).

Virtually every culture and civilization in history has been aware of and believed in the reality of invisible beings, good and bad. There is a tremendous world of spirits around us that people are not aware of. This is a realm of angels.

Houston, my home town, is a big old city with millions of people. The population stands somewhere around 3.5 million. As I walk into a city, I instantly bind the "prince of the air," principalities and power and rulers of darkness and religious spirits in high places that control the airwaves.

Man's immediate future will bring an increasing involvement with supernatural powers, both good and evil, but I believe it is imperative for our generation to be fully acquainted with real and genuine supernaturalism, as well as the false and evil. God's word tells us that angels are real and that their duty is to minister to the heirs of salvation. What a mighty God we serve.

Chapter 39

Espionage Has Rules?

We were back in Moscow; it was 1990. We were given our favorite personalized taxi driver to carry us wherever we needed to go. His name was Valentine. We had met on one of our earlier tours, and we were more acquainted. I met Sokalov for the very first time in Houston at Lakewood Church. The pastor, John Osteen from Lakewood Church, had invited representatives from the Moscow Baptist Church and appointed special laymen to look after them. In this case it was oilman Andy SoRelle Jr. who called me and ask me to take them out to dinner and he would bear the expense. Andy's dad was a pioneer wildcatter back in the early 1900's and one of the richest. You might say that Andy Jr. had everything in life growing up. I took Sokalov and three other Russians to Steve Christie, Christie's Seafood to eat. Steve is always jolly and cordially suggested the most expensive dish on the menu. Steve is a very kind, giving man.

The Russian Sokalov spoke English, and he was asking me to come to Moscow and hold a crusade. He would get the Russian Baptist Church to pay our hotel and food expenses. The time had arrived to return to Moscow, and I took them to the airport and got them upgraded to first class from tourist and placed them in the President's Club with Continental Airlines. They were all so over-grateful and could not understand how I did this; Sokalov had thought maybe I was with the CIA, just as I thought he was with the KGB. The Premier in Russia was still Gorbachev at that time.

When I arrived in Moscow, the weather was atrocious cold and drizzle rain. I was hoping someone was going to pick us up. Sokalov had sent Valentine to pick me up, hoping to return some of the V.I.P. treatment we had given him. The next day, I was able to take Sokalov to the western Irish mini-supermarket to buy him U.S. fresh meat and canned goods he needed. He was so thrilled and later we helped repaint the church that he pastored and helped feed the poor. In fact this church became a soup kitchen for the needy and served hundreds of meals weekly. We also made a memorial to Dr. and Mary King, who helped remodel this church. (This special lady made this all possible; Mary King gave us $50,000.00 in 1990 to make our thrust into Russia and Siberia, Riga, Latvia, and an open door on television to preach Christ over the old U.S.S.R.)

Thank God for obedient vessels that sacrifice to get the Gospel out throughout the world. Here are a few we will always be grateful to our Lord for. One of the great soul winners who helped us over the years is Joan Dupler; she gave $25,000. What blessings this ministry has received from saints such as Oliver Bivins, giving $2000 monthly for years; then the oil crises came and he retired. I think about Mary Stephens that gave this soul-winning work nearly a half-million dollars to get us started over a seven-year plan in the 70's. What about Pat Robertson, who sacrificed to win souls $100,000 for crusades. What more can I say about the monthly givers who have been faithful? Cherylyn Boyd from Indiana, Norman Norwood. One of the best personal injury attorneys in the country, James Manley, through a gift of a bargain, sale, donation, gave us a building downtown and a shopping center. I have been in real estate all of my life and therefore had the experience to put a new facelift and sell them. Later after eighteen months, I sold the building for $360,000 and the shopping center for additional $200,000 more than I paid for it. This gave us $560,000 for evangelism. I did not put this money in a C.D. for us personally but used it all for television and crusades and the ministry. I could have taken a $100,000, paid taxes and put in a retirement account for us. But I left it in the mission fund.

Then in 1988 when nearly everyone was hurt financially in Texas, it was the Attorney James Manly who bailed us out by taking over the shopping center. God Bless James Manley. Then William Morris

III and wonderful Sharon gave us $25,000 for missions. In the eighties Wedded Haddad, a Palestinian mother, gave $30,000 for three crusades, one crusade for each of her children: Ghassan, Nizar, and Rima Haddad. Wedded has been a blessing to this day.

The story behind Johnny Mitchell Sr. deserves a chapter of its own. Johnny was Johnny, there has never been anyone like Johnny. He gave us $28,000 one year and a note for $5000. Norman Dobbins at the same time gave a promissory note for one year for $5000. One year later I saw Johnny and briefly mentioned the note; he said renew it. He went on to pay it later. He was only kidding. I went to intensive care six years after to pray for Johnny Mitchell, and when I looked at him, I asked the Lord to have mercy on him and remember all the good Johnny did on this earth and spare his life. It was Johnny that gave me a word of good reference and co-signed my first note for $2500. Later Johnny said, "Chris, you are one of the only few that ever paid his note off." Johnny is in Heaven now. Please pray for his sweet wife, Aileen Mitchell. Johnny was a prince of a man to all who knew him.

Earnestine and I thank you all. The Lord has given us some of the best soul winners and the best givers in the world. It has been a hard 7 years, and sometimes we have thought we were not going to make it. The Lord is our Source and we shall not want. My mind drifted back to Russia; we had been told that Valentine was also assigned to Billy Graham when he was in Moscow.

Earnestine and I had flown into Moscow for another speaking engagement. Upon arrival, we contacted the Baptist Church as usual, asking for a driver that could pick us up and deliver us to our hotel. They obligingly sent Valentine.

"So good to see you again, Mr. and Mrs. Panos. Where have you been?" asked Valentine with his usual smile.

"All around the world, India, China, and many other places since we last saw you," I said, grabbing his hand. We were beginning to look forward to seeing Valentine.

We bounded into our busy schedule of meetings. So much was going on that it was a few days before Earnestine made the comment.

"It seems strange. If you need your suit pressed or cleaned, or a replacement for something you've lost, Valentine appears as if on cue. If we are hungry and discussing ordering something, he appears and takes us out to dinner. He must have a sixth sense!"

I thought on her statement. Espionage has rules. Rule number one, never blow your cover. Making a motion with my hands, I asked Earnestine to get a pencil, and I handed her a pad. I motioned for her to write down whatever she was going to say to me. Her expression was questioning, but she soon caught on.

Over the next week we made a game of it. When we needed to discuss something of importance, we wrote it down. Communicating with each other on important matters via the written word. Strangely enough, we found out that Valentine suddenly lost his sixth sense.

I was always consistent in scrutinizing situations, but for some reason this trip, it had taken me a little longer to realize that our room was being bugged.

The following day the entire top floor of our hotel was taken over by Chinese from Mainland, Red China. They seemed to be lurking around every corner.

Valentine was so likable, with a giving heart. From this little test, we now knew that he was a KGB operative. We were saddened by the thought—not only that our friend involved with the KGB, but also that the Baptist Church had sent him to us. I spent hours quoting Scriptures and loving him, and I believe God is doing a work in him. I was confronted only with KGB agents at the beginning of my ministry. There was so much love in Valentine, and I know if he had the chance he would go all the way with Christ.

One morning days later, after driving us places and following us around, taking care of all our needs, and listening to us share Christ, he waited purposely to speak to us as we were standing beside our car. The questioning was directed in a purposeful way. I would have believed he had a changed personality. He asked, "How can I learn more about this man named Jesus Christ?"

There was a sincerity in his voice that had not been there before. Was it coincidental that he had chosen a spot where there was no hidden microphone?

I edged closer, looking directly into his eyes. "Jesus is the appointed one from God. You know about appointments, don't you?" I asked. He nodded that he did. "Well, Jesus has been waiting for you to keep that appointment with Him."

He looked reflective. For the next few minutes I shared God's message with Valentine.

"Can I ask Jesus into my heart? Would it be okay?" he asked with great sincerity. Right there outside our car, on that bright sunny morning, he offered up one of the most genuine and awesome humbling prayers I have ever heard. It was not eloquent, but neither was Valentine. It was quick and meaningful, and I knew that Valentine had made his peace with God.

What started out as a surface friendship became deeply rooted by our common bond. Too bad I did not feel the same about Menshikov. Speaking of which, I had not seen him for some time now.

"Where is Menshikov?" I asked Valentine. His eyes shifted cautiously. "I am told he has been traveling and will be starting his own work, leaving the Baptist Church."

Chapter 40

I Almost Didn't Go

The alpha, or the beginning of my ministry, I totally surrendered my life to the Lord. I had never given that much of my life to any cause before. Looking back now, I realize it was the biggest of all miracles God performed.

It was September 1992; my mind was on weighty matters, matters to do with the Lord's work. Every day I was more burdened for my ministry's future. Money was getting scarce. A whole set of new economic woes were hitting America. The TV evangelism atrocities, a direct move of Satan, had created a lack of confidence in Christian ethics. The America people were questioning and withdrawing from donating money for anything. Like we are still there, in today's climate. It is the ministry that appears before the people daily that get the most finances. It is sad but true. Our people on our mailing list are getting old and going on to be with the Lord. Advertising tells us that you must add new names to your list daily to replace the ones who have died. The ministry on TV and churches have the best opportunity to get these new Christian names and add them to their list. If you are not traveling in the Churches and appearing on television or have a TV program, you are not getting the chance to get these new believers on your list. The Lord performs miracles of finance, but when you are before millions of people it is easier for the Lord to touch one of these precious people. Nevertheless, let God be true and every man a liar. Our God is able to do it with a thousand people. He can do anything, anytime, any way He wants to.

Today Christian ethics are on the firing line more than ever.

Over the next few pages are the closing chapters of my book. They aren't, however, the closing chapters of my Christian life. Whenever the devil slips in to rob and destroy, a new method of ministry will be birthed.

I was increasingly burdened to go to Albania, one of the most godless nations of that region. Finances were at an all-time low. I was almost walking in the same shoes I had in the first years of my ministry. I was having to go back to being a totally dependent on the Lord. I knew God has a plan in all things and the God of heaven; He will prosper us.

The Bible entreats us daily to take up the cross and not look back—not to the past and what was done before, or to our abilities, or material things of life. Like manna from heaven we must get our needs met daily through the grace set up for each of us.

Because of the money situation, I was heading into Albania on the cheapest ticket. I knew this was God's plan and trip. I had been in God's business too long not to believe that something very special was about to happen. God was working a special grace in my life.

My first stop was Thessalonika, Greece. It had been fourteen years since I had been back. For years I had been making attempts to get *God's Spy* translated into Greek, but it had not yet materialized.

The book has been published in Chinese, German, Spanish, Norwegian, Finish, Danish, and more. I met Spiro Zodiathes, to whom I gave *God's Spy*. He translated the Bible recently from Greek to English with a simple help study. He was in Houston just last week. He wrote me a thank you for *God's Spy*: "I will treasure the book and meeting you the rest of my life." Spiro was arrested and spent five years in prison charged with proselytizing in Greece. In the Greek constitution it says it is against the law to proselytize against the Greek Orthodox Church. He was a great inspiration to many. Now the opportunity is here to get *God's Spy* translated into Greek and offered to all the Greek-speaking people in the world. We are praying for the right contact. I believe it is God's timing for the Greeks to read *God's Spy*.

Most of my trip had been planned for me. My first Church meeting was in Thessalonika, Greece, located on the southernmost part of the Balkan Peninsula on the Aegean Sea. Just a few hundred miles lies Macedonia and the Bosnian war. The Greek people are ready to go to war. The air was electric with war. These thoughts were pulsating in my being. I flew into the area in the early hours of the morning. What a breathtaking view, Thessalonika at sunrise. An ancient geographer once wrote, "The sea presses in upon the country with a thousand arms." Everywhere the eye could lay fingers of dark green waters that seemed to intimately caress the seascape. It was an emotional meeting for me, coming back to my origins after fourteen years. In the past the place had been so very poor, but now everything was booming.

Looking out across the expanse of hills, the Pineus range, and scanning the rugged and sparsely populated areas, I remembered stories of my childhood. Central and Southern Greece, shaped like a giant hand with impassable mountain peaks, extends out like fingers into sea, and the rugged ridges run down into the narrow valleys isolated from the other, but open to the sea. The valleys were beautiful. Likewise were the people who lived in them.

I'm not sure why, but it all reminded me of my own meager beginnings down along the Texas seacoast of Galveston.

Apart from the fact that Greece lays claim to being the cradle of Democracy, it is also the birthplace of Alexander The Great, and the land of legend and beauty which has inspired centuries of art and philosophy. They are courageous people and naturally friendly, offering all visitors a warm and hearty welcome.

The first night I was scheduled to preach at the fellowship. It's not a church, but a separate group of businessmen who happen to be a part of the Greek Orthodox Church. I felt led to preach about the heart. The altar was filled with people, literally crowded in the aisles, tears flowing, people coming to know and coming to get back to Christ, renewing their pledge from years past. When I speak of emotional times and tears, please do not take it lightly. I don't. I know it is God's Holy Spirit doing a work in the heart of every man, woman, and every boy and girl.

On Sunday morning the people attend the Greek Orthodox Church. On Sunday night they gather in a fellowship service. People wanting to hear me came from north, and south, east and west of Greece. In Greece if you have several hundred it is considered a large meeting. The crowd had swollen until there was no more room. The theater was packed, people drawn by the Holy Spirit to hear God's Word.

I believe this is the beginning of great revival that will birth very soon in Greece.

Chapter 41

Our Sparks Ignited

"I have someone here who would like to meet you, Chris," said Mario. "This is Marco Pappas."

I smiled and listened to the formal introduction. He was a nice-looking young man whom I found out later was a very devoted Christian. It was spontaneous. Our sparks instantly ignited.

"I've wanted to meet someone like you for a long time, Mr. Panos," he said as he stuck out an eager hand.

He smiled, forgetting anything he might have rehearsed. I was sure he had never done this sort of thing before, but he was enthusiastic and had control of English as well.

"I have heard about you, Mr. Panos, heard about you and your ministry. I made this trip from far away just in hopes to meet you." He look reflective. "I would give anything to be a part of your team." The words came with deep conviction; I was overjoyed with surprise. I'd never laid eyes on this man before and here he was making such a request. His openness was an admirable trait, especially for God's work.

"Well, if you are in the market? I need an overseas director," I tossed back.

"I'm not experienced in that, but if you would want me, I would be willing."

I looked him in the eye, my words never faltering. "God impressed on me that he would be sending someone, but he asked that I 'wait' 'til he showed me the man for the position."

Marco Pappas flashed a winning smile. "If I pass your test, be assured that I would do my best."

It did not take long into our conversation and I knew this was a meeting that was prearranged from God, for the young man to approach me at this time. Like the three youths that became couriers at the Moscow University, I could envision what a team we could make. For years I'd been accepting the Lord's leading in such manner. At that moment I felt obliged to accept his offer. He thanked me graciously. We felt an immediate kinship.

"Thank you, Lord," I said under my breath for another miracle. No one but the Lord Himself could have possibly known how much I needed this. I've found over the years that when I have a need, I offer up my petition, then leave it in God's capable hands.

If in my humanness my judgment has been blinded, and the request is not in his perfect timing and desire, it seems to get lost in the asking.

Marco received word that one of his aunts in Germany was gravely sick, possibly about to die. He made a call to the family.

"How would you like to fly with me to East Berlin?" he asked purposely after the call. I must have appeared hesitant. "My family extends a special invitation to you. They would pay your ticket."

I smiled. "Then book a flight, Marco," I said.

"It's been a while since I have been to East Berlin." I believe I was sent there to minister to the family, but while I was there, I wanted to try and set up a future crusade.

From Germany we flew directly into Albania, a harsh land with craggy mountains and rushing streams. You might see a young shepherd playing his flute-like pan pipe, watching this flock. If you ask the young man where he lives, he probably would reply, "In the Land of Eagles."

When we flew into Albania, Marco had no visa and neither did I. This certainly had not been part of the plan. I had a multiple visa for Mainland China and Russia that in the past you could use for Albania. As we approached customs, I handed him mine. If he was going to be my overseas director, it was time he got started.

"I'm sorry," he said to customs, "this quick trip was not in the plan, but I need a visa. We have a business to tend to there." His words were convincing. Time and experience would groom him, I thought.

"Allow me to break in," I said. I knew I had to use tact, but also boldness. I call it bulldog tactics—use the Name of Jesus as battleaxe to open the door if need be. I showed him a picture of George Bush, the President of the United States, and myself. I knew James Baker, the Secretary of State, recently was there and addressed three hundred thousand people in Tirana, Albania. The customs guard was taken by surprise, and his face broke out in a smile, and he began speaking in Albanian several others standing around him. They ordered the guard to walk us through the customs after stamping our passports. I knew it was getting dark and read about the mass hijacking going on in Albanian, and I felt better to travel in the daylight. It turned pitch dark within thirty minutes, and I began binding the prince of the air in Albania and the special cab driver as we traveled over one and one half hours to the hotel in Tirana, the capital.

I had sent a request for a room in the best hotel they had in Tirana. The hotel was built by Mussolini, the dictator of Italy, during the Second World War. It was old but nice. There were people bustling around the lobby the taxi driver brought our luggage in and stayed with us as I spoke to the desk clerk seeking a room, and after thirty minutes of bargaining and after hearing the same story, "we have no room for you," again and again.

I told him I have an American shirt and tie with US flag on it. He went crazy and began to drool. I then asked for a suite, knowing that instead of two separate rooms we could rent a suite and Marco could sleep in the living room part of the suite. The desk clerk said, "I have a suite but it is $95.00 each night with no discount." The rent on two separate rooms were a higher rate this way and I would save 40%. I took the suite with great joy because only God knew what else was available and I was with Marco and I wanted to shelter him. The desk clerk slammed his hand on a bell and bellhop came and took our luggage as we stepped our way inch by inch through the traffic which was horrendous in the lobby. The smoke in the lobby reminded me of London, being caught up in the fog. Everyone butting against everyone else people speaking Greek, Italian, German, American. Entrepreneurs from many nations were trying to make some money. We got to the elevator, and it was so small that we barely got on it with all the luggage. The elevator bounced a couple of times on the way up. It reminded me to keep praying fervently.

We checked into the room and the maid came in right away to help us get settled. I noticed that her hand was bandaged and swollen. I said, "Have you taken any penicillin?"

She laughed out loud, then began to weep. "I wish there was some penicillin. I have been only drinking some alcohol when the fever comes."

I remember Dr. Carroll West had given me several bottles of medicine. I told her to let me pray for her and she was very open and then I led her to Christ. I could tell the Lord was in her heart; she reflected such peace in her appearance. I said to her, "Take this package of penicillin. There are twenty one tablets; take one every six hours." This is what Dr. West told me to tell them. She was beside herself and began to kiss my hand as though I was a Father in the Greek Orthodox Church. I told her that it was not necessarily, just go home and start taking the pills. I asked directions to the main hospital and she told us. She scooted out the door happy. I told Marco tomorrow we'd go to the hospital and give them the aspirins, penicillin and several other antibiotics I had brought from the America.

The next day we found the hospital and Dr. Gen. Bashk, and he led us to the main pharmacy. I gave the medicines to the nurses, and they were beside themselves. One said, "You will never know what this medicine means to us." I had some samples of perfume given to me from the Estee Lauder manager in Galleria's Marshall Fields and I passed them out to the nurses.

Then Doctor Bashk said, "I wish I had one for my girlfriend." I gave him one.

I said, "Marco, go to the Ministry of the Government and get me an appointment with the President." Marco was astounded and remarked they will not listen to me. I encouraged him they would, and the door opened to meet with several key officials. One of them was Artan Hoxhan, Minister of Trade and Foreign Economic Corporation of the Republic of Albania. He assured me if the President was in the country, he would have made time to see me.

Another door opened to Ministry of tourism and Ministry of the stadium that we leased for a future date for a crusade. The President wants the nation of Albania to convert from Islam to Christianity. I have the chance to hold a crusade in Albania in 1995 or 1996. I believe with God's help and yours, all of this will be made possible. The time is short. Please stand with us to reach Albania.

Marco and I, after a great dinner that night, left the next day for Greece. We returned to Thessalonika. Mario the Pastor had set up a seminar for me to speak. It was great. Then Marco heard I was going to India very soon and wanted to come with me to India.

I told him to ask the church to pray with him and his family. Costa and Maria, his brother in-law and a sister, found a way for him to get passage.

Chapter 42

The Last Challenge

Of all the crusades that I have held in India, the one in Nagpur stands out most vividly in my mind. Perhaps the reason Nagpur still seems so vivid is because it was the last I held before the book *God's Spy* was finished.

Enormous crowds and innumerable miracles made the Nagpur crusade an overwhelming success. The mayor of Nagpur, B.M. Gailkwad, came out to meet me at the airport, enormous crowds massed to hear the gospel, and even the Indian newsmen gave the Nagpur crusade outstanding coverage. This was a miracle in itself, since their Hindu-owned newspapers are usually quite hostile to the Gospel.

The Nagpur crusade started on a Thursday. Early, early in the morning, the crowds began to gather at the Kasturchand Park Ground, waiting patiently in the hot Indian sun for the time when the evening crusade would start. An Indian filmmaker volunteered to make a movie of the crusade.

Early in the crusade, I taught the people to praise the Lord. The crowed stood, and following our instructions, they raised their hands. The field was about six hundred yards long and about three hundred and fifty yards wide. As the people stood waving their outstretched hands in praise, they reminded me of a gigantic wheat field. I understood what Jesus had meant when He talked of "fields white to harvest."

On the first night of the crusade, a Malayan lady, the wife of a driver in the fire brigade, brought two of her four children to the platform. Her two sons had been born deaf and dumb. Her husband had given up all hope of his sons ever being able to talk, but when we tested the ten-year-old, young Jay Prakash, he admitted he could hear. His astounded mother burst into tears. Her other son was healed as well.

Another ear healing that night was a Sikh lady, the wife of a building contractor, who had not been able to hear from her left ear for the past three years.

"I tried practically every hospital, both in Nagpur and in Delhi," she testified. "I was undergoing treatment, but nothing had helped. When I heard of this meeting, I came hoping for a miracle. Now I have hearing in both ears."

Other ear healings included a forty-five-year-old tailor from the Sadar area who had been deaf in one ear, and a medical doctor in the government hospital in Chandrapur. He had tried every treatment that he knew without success, but within minutes of arriving at the meeting, he could hear clearly with both ears. He was so moved he could hardly express his joy.

In addition to the many ear healings in Nagpur, there were other miracles of all descriptions. Growths and tumors disappeared, cripples walked, and the demon-possessed were freed and saved. And as always, multitudes accepted Jesus Christ, which is the greatest miracle of all.

The Nagpur crusade started on a Thursday. Crowds built quickly on Friday and Saturday. "And the next Sabbath day" (to quote Acts 13:44) "came almost the whole city together to hear the word of God." Attendance was estimated at over one hundred thousand on Sunday alone, and many thousands were saved and healed. Again, there were too many miracles for us to count. But no matter how many miracles I had in Nagpur, no matter how many miracles I have in any city, it will not be enough. That is why I wrote several books: to challenge you, the reader, to go into all the world and preach the gospel.

The gospel witness that Jesus Christ is the Son of God is the most important news of any day. When it first was heard, it spread like wildfire as the presence of God's Holy Spirit—indwelling fishermen, farmers, tent makers, and civil servants, turning men with hearts of flesh into flaming, burning evangelists who pointed the masses toward the only source of salvation: Jesus Christ, the Son of the Living God.

This same power is available to you. With God's power, you too can reach all the nations of the world. There are no closed doors to the gospel. And God wants you to go.

As I write this, the field lies white to harvest, like the harvest field in Nagpur. The world lies dying, poisoned by sin. The antidote is Jesus. You may not be called the way I was to tell His story. You do not need some kind of special vision. God is already waiting for you to meet the challenge. And He has already issued you your marching orders: "Go ye into all the world, and preach the gospel to every creature" (Mark 16:15).

Go ye.

* * *